THE EMPTY
KINGDOM

Novels by Elizabeth E. Wein

THE MARK OF SOLOMON
THE LION HUNTER (BOOK ONE)
THE EMPTY KINGDOM (BOOK TWO)

THE SUNBIRD

A COALITION OF LIONS

THE WINTER PRINCE

THE EMPTY KINGDOM

THE MARK OF SOLOMON ~ BOOK TWO

ELIZABETH E. WEIN

VIKING

VIKING
Published by Penguin Group
Penguin Group (USA) Inc., 345 Hudson Street, New York, New York 10014, U.S.A.
Penguin Group (Canada), 90 Eglinton Avenue East, Suite 700, Toronto, Ontario, Canada M4P 2Y3
(a division of Pearson Penguin Canada Inc.)
Penguin Books Ltd, 80 Strand, London WC2R 0RL, England
Penguin Ireland, 25 St Stephen's Green, Dublin 2, Ireland (a division of Penguin Books Ltd)
Penguin Group (Australia), 250 Camberwell Road, Camberwell, Victoria 3124, Australia
(a division of Pearson Australia Group Pty Ltd)
Penguin Books India Pvt Ltd, 11 Community Centre, Panchsheel Park, New Delhi—110 017, India
Penguin Group (NZ), 67 Apollo Drive, Rosedale,
North Shore 0632, New Zealand (a division of Pearson New Zealand Ltd.)
Penguin Books (South Africa) (Pty) Ltd, 24 Sturdee Avenue, Rosebank, Johannesburg 2196, South Africa

Penguin Books Ltd, Registered Offices: 80 Strand, London WC2R 0RL, England

First published in 2008 by Viking, a member of Penguin Group (USA) Inc.

1   3   5   7   9   10   8   6   4   2

Text and map copyright © Elizabeth Gatland, 2008
All rights reserved

"Mu'Allaqa of Tarafa," from The Seven Odes, translated by A. J. Arberry (London: George Allen and Unwin, 1957).
An online version of The Seven Odes is available at www.muslimphilosophy.com/books/odes.pdf

Grateful thanks to Katherine Jarman and my dear friend Helen Sanders Fray,
for their efforts in translating enough ancient Greek to allow me to compose
the sonnet in "The Sealed Agreement" on Goewin's behalf.

LIBRARY OF CONGRESS CATALOGING-IN-PUBLICATION DATA
Wein, Elizabeth.
The empty kingdom : the mark of Solomon book II / Elizabeth E. Wein.
p. cm.
Sequel to: The lion hunter.
Summary: Telemakos, imprisoned on the upper levels of Abreha's, ruler of Himyar, twelve-story palace and lacking
any way to communicate his predicament to his family in far-away Aksum, tries to find a subtle and effective way to
regain his freedom.
ISBN 978-0-670-06273-7 (hardcover)
[1. Prisoners—Fiction. 2. Kings, queens, rulers, etc.—Fiction. 3. Interpersonal relations—Fiction. 4. Arabia,
Southern—History—6th century—Fiction. 5. Aksum (Kingdom)—Fiction.] I. Title.
PZ7.W4358Em 2008
[Fic]—dc22
2007029082

Printed in U.S.A.   Set in Goudy Old Style   Book design by Jim Hoover

The publisher does not have any control over and does not assume any responsibility
for author or third-party Web sites or their content.

For Christopher Marcus Santos
(because before Telemakos, there was Chris)

THE EMPTY
KINGDOM

Contents

THE ARABIAN PENINSULA

"Set me as a seal upon your heart,
as a seal upon your arm;
for love is strong as death."

~SONG OF SOLOMON 8:6

I

LETTERS TO AFRICA

THE RED SEA had never seemed so wide, nor Aksum so far away.

To the Lady Turunesh Kidane, my darling mother, greetings.

I don't think I've told you yet, Mother, for I am ashamed to admit it, but I am once again in disgrace for listening at doors. As punishment I am confined to my workplace for this entire season, and not allowed to see my sister, or any of the other children in the palace. Abreha Anbessa the Lion Hunter, Abreha najashi and mukarrib, king of Himyar and federator of all the Arabs of the Coastal Plains—

Telemakos used the najashi's full formal title, just for effect. Abreha would insist on reading the letter himself before he allowed it to be sent on its long journey home.

—The najashi requires me to wear a bracelet of bells and charms that ring when I move. It's an alarm, to warn people I am there. Grandfather and all the imperial court will say I deserve it, and that it should have been done long ago.

He had worn it for two weeks now, and already it seemed endless.

Telemakos was kept under guard in the Great Globe Room, where he had studied and slept since coming to Himyar eight months ago, and the adjoining scriptorium, where the najashi's maps and books were kept. These rooms were on the highest level of Maharis Ghumdan, the tiered alabaster palaces supposed to have been built by Solomon. The only higher place you could climb to was the narrow parapet around the domed roof of the Great Globe Room, where the ancient water clock dripped and chimed.

Telemakos was allowed to leave the scriptorium for two hours each morning when he joined the najashi's young spearmen for their daily practice in the training grounds. He could see all San'a city from his window, and the al-Surat Mountains that ringed the plain, but all he saw of Abreha's vast palace were its endless flights of marble stairs, twelve stories down and twelve stories back up, taken every day at a forced march under the indifferent gaze of Abreha's guardsmen.

Telemakos could see no end to this season of disgrace. When his imprisonment was over, he would still have to wear the alarm bells, and in case Telemakos should dare to cross

him, the najashi had already written out his death warrant—
truly, a death warrant, an order for Telemakos's execution. It
was real. It was sealed with the ancient star and lion signet of
King Solomon and a lock of Telemakos's own distinctive hair,
inherited from his British father and pale as bone, unmistak-
ably identifying Telemakos and no one else. Abreha kept the
warrant bound in his waistband.

When Telemakos wanted to send a letter to his family,
Abreha required him to read it aloud in his presence, to make
sure Telemakos was not reporting Himyar's secrets to the imperial city of Aksum. Telemakos feared and hated these sessions
in the najashi's study so deeply that the apprehension of them
was beginning to corrupt his life. In spite of the warrant that
Abreha carried in his sash, Telemakos was determined to send a
warning to his emperor through the letters he sent to his mother,
and he had a plan for doing it. But his success depended on slow
patience. He would be killed if he was caught.

What madness, Telemakos thought, that my parents sent
me here to keep me safe.

He had already written a letter each to his mother and
his aunt Goewin and mentioned nothing. He was especially
careful about anything he sent to Goewin anyway, for she was
Britain's ambassador to Aksum and must not be revealed as
the emperor Gebre Meskal's private counselo . *Queen of spies*,
Telemakos's father had called her. Before Telemakos's disgrace
he had written to her weekly, and he could not suddenly begin
to write more often without arousing suspicion. But a fortnight

had passed since he had become aware of Abreha's treachery, and Telemakos was beginning to feel that time was crumbling to dust beneath his feet. He could not afford to wait much longer with his warning; it took six weeks, at best, for his letters to reach home.

How did I ever think it was hard being the child of an African mother and a British father? Telemakos wondered. It is *nothing* compared to living in Himyar and owing allegiance to Aksum. I feel as though I am being dragged to pieces by elephants.

Hide your secrets, Turunesh had told him just before he had come to Himyar. *Write to me that you send your love to your aunt, and code your meaning following your greeting to her.*

How do I code it? How do I write it? A letter to my mother, nothing could be more straightforward. So how do I hide in it that Abreha the Lion Hunter is plotting against his cousin, the emperor of Aksum? Dearest Mother: The najashi means to infiltrate the emperor's navy with Himyar's soldiers, to create a mutiny, to seize our Hanish Islands for their wealth of obsidian and pearls, to free the exiles and smugglers imprisoned there. Dearest Mother: Your neighbor Gedar is an informer and a traitor to the emperor. How do I say it? Which shall I tackle first: mutiny, invasion, or smuggling? God help me.

Telemakos wrote:

Pass on my love to my father, and to Grandfather, and to my aunt Goewin. Our little Athena would send her love as well, if she were old enough to consider such things.

As he wrote, Telemakos pressed so hard on the reed stylus that he snapped off the point. He did this all the time. The narrow strips of palm were inexpensive to write on but practically impossible for him to manage now with his single arm. Athena, nearly two years old, had learned to hold down the tapes for him.

Telemakos rubbed his eyes angrily. He could not write or speak his sister's name without wanting to weep. He did not know how he could endure an entire season of being separated from her, knowing she was there, just one story below. At night he could hear her snoring through the pulley hole in the floor of the Great Globe Room. He could always hear her when she cried, even when he retreated to the scriptorium, even from the roof.

He slept every night on the floor, with his head hanging over the shaft to the nursery. Twice a day he could watch Athena playing, or more usually throwing tantrums, on the terrace below the Globe Room's eastern windows. She spotted him up there once and caused pandemonium by trying to scale the balcony to get to him. When one of Abreha's royal foster children pulled her back, Athena grabbed hold of Inas's face with both hands and tore scratches in her cheeks.

Telemakos let the strip of palm curl up. He would have to practice his message in wax first, so that he could rub out his false starts. He chewed on his knuckles, still wondering where to begin. His fingers tasted of salt where he had scrubbed at the shameful tears: bitter, bitter.

Salt, Telemakos thought. He could start with salt. The salt

smuggling was over, at any rate. It was nearly a year since Gebre Meskal had lifted the plague quarantine that the najashi had ignored. Perhaps, Telemakos thought, perhaps this old news is irrelevant enough that Abreha will forgive me if he finds me passing it along.

Telemakos scratched into a wax tablet:

Abreha ignored the quarantine.
He was the smugglers' chieftain and championed the unfair
exchange in salt.
He seeks—

He seeks me, Telemakos thought, chewing at his knuckles again. He's hunting down the emperor's spies. The najashi does not know it, but the ruin of his smuggling ring at the Afar mines was all my doing. What shall I say he seeks? One of my code names—sunbird, harrier, python?

Telemakos heard in memory the quiet voice of Aksum's young emperor Gebre Meskal, murmuring at his ear: *No man must ever know the true name of my sunbird.*

Telemakos could not write his secret name. He could scarcely bring himself to speak it aloud anymore, not since the day when they had found a real sunbird nailed to the gate of his grandfather's house like a curse or a sacrifice; and anyway, Telemakos did not dare to flourish Aksumite imperial code in a letter the najashi would read. He wrote simply:

Abreha seeks Gebre Meskal's secret keeper from that time.

I'll break these phrases apart, he thought, and hide the words among a lot of other nonsense, and give Goewin some clue how to pick up the key words. What if I try to put two words of my message after each mention of Athena's name?

He rubbed out a few words to make his challenge briefer.

And then when I have to read the thing aloud to the najashi, Telemakos decided, I'll make up something outrageous to say at the end that I haven't really written, to distract him from the real message.

Telemakos shivered. For a moment he put his head down on the worktop, resting his cheek against the cool and shining ebony and rubbing at his burning eyes. If Abreha caught on to the damning encoded message, he would bring out the parchment folded in his sash, break the mark of Solomon and discard the telltale strands of Telemakos's thick hair that were threaded through the page, and pass the execution order on to his lieutenant.

Could I argue coincidence if he accuses me of duplicity? Telemakos considered, and read over again his etched words:

Abreha ignored quarantine
championed unfair exchange
Abreha seeks Gebre Meskal's secret keeper

There is no idiot alive who would believe this is coincidence, once he worked it out, Telemakos thought grimly. I had better get it right.

It took him three days to put it together. All the time he worked on it, he was scarcely able to make himself eat, he was so sick with the dread of having to present it to Abreha.

"Drop that," Dawit Alta'ir, the Star Master, barked at him as Telemakos wrote. Dawit slapped the stylus from Telemakos's grip. The alarm bells chattered. "You are ruining that tablet."

Telemakos had been plowing furrows through the wax, lost in the composition of a sentence that he did not yet dare to write down. Dawit might be nearly blinded by cataracts, but the grooves Telemakos had made in the tablet laid bare the wood beneath, making deep, dark streaks that anyone could have seen from across the room.

"Put your work away. You may wipe the dust off the things in the compass cabinet. That will give you something to do with your body and free your mind to wander." Dawit picked a kat leaf out of his wild beard, nibbled at it, and spat it out. Telemakos swallowed a sigh; it was one of his duties to keep the floor clean.

"Your pardon, Magus," Telemakos murmured, trying to shovel the wax back into place.

They had diplomatically set aside the work of preserving what Abreha called the Plague Tablets, the unfinished maps of the disputed Hanish Islands. Telemakos dreaded being asked, or compelled, to complete the project that would bring about war between Aksum and Himyar. He did not know how he could bring himself to do it faithfully, or without dragging out the work to excessive lengths to buy time, and it was an immense relief when Dawit Alta'ir set him to other tasks.

When his letter was ready, Telemakos rattled downstairs toward Abreha's apartment, in awe at his own resolution. His two guards followed at his heels. What is driving me to tell this to Goewin? Telemakos marveled. I have only to keep it to myself, and I will be safe. Why am I compelled to spill it all? If I get away with it, I will do it again, I'll tell them as much as I can. In every letter I send home now, I risk my life—why am I doing it?

Abreha's doorman admitted Telemakos. Telemakos stood before the najashi. He kept his head bowed, not daring to look the najashi in the face, but he knew that Abreha gazed frowning down at him from beneath his heavy, forbidding brow.

"I want to send a letter to my mother."

The najashi held forth his hand to usher Telemakos into his study. It always shocked Telemakos how like the emperor Gebre Meskal's hands the najashi's hands were, narrow and neat and dark, the palms cool and dry when you touched them. But of course the najashi and the emperor were cousins, countrymen; Abreha was Aksumite by birth, raised on the African side of the Red Sea, like Telemakos. He had been elected to his status as federator of South Arabia, not born to it.

"Let me hear your letter."

Telemakos was so practiced in evasive deception that he did not even pause for breath when his carefully constructed greeting to his mother made its crucial turn.

"Send my love to my aunt. Now I'm going to the window to watch my sister crawling about the terrace below. I watch after Athena whenever she appears, twice every day, in the morning and again immediately after her noon meal; twice each day I follow Athena with my gaze, and silently send her the love that I also send you.

"I haven't told you much about my punishment. It's difficult for the baby as well, indeed for all the household, and I didn't want to worry you. For this entire season I am not allowed near Athena. Abreha ignored my previous small wrongdoings, but this time I explored the contents of his own desk, though I did it only because the baby thought there would be pictures in it that she liked. So now I am separated from Athena, quarantine championed by the najashi to stop me committing any more disobedience on her behalf.

"I knew what I was doing, but she didn't. Poor bewildered Athena; unfair exchange, to ask your brother's help and then be forbidden to see him again! But although I can't come near Athena, Abreha seeks her company and plays with her and ensures she gets plenty of affection and amusement.

"Sometimes I long for home. Will I ever be able to show Athena Gebre Meskal's new lion pit? Will she feel at home there, as I did once? Will she hide among the palms of the Golden Court, as I did, watching the courtiers—will she become, my Athena, secret keeper of all imperial gossip, as I did long ago?

"I read over these questions and to my surprise I find they make me laugh. I hope she doesn't grow up as outrageously behaved as I!

"How I miss you, my dear family: my father, and Grandfather, and Goewin, and you, Mother, more than all.

"The first month of my correction is half finished, as I've written. I apologize for having made so much complaint in this letter, but I am under sentence of death if I tell anyone what I learned from the najashi."

Abreha's censor's brush was poised and dripping.

"*Give me that.* Our covenant is private between us. That letter will be in the hands of half a dozen couriers over the next six weeks, and you risk all of Himyar learning its contents! You've scratched it in palm, have you? It will show through the ink if I paint over it. You will have to cut that last sentence out, or rewrite it."

Telemakos handed him the letter. He watched as Abreha skimmed quickly through the writing. The najashi's heavy brow and keen black gaze were familiar to him now, but even more so the dark and narrow hands holding the palm strip, for Telemakos never dared meet the najashi's eyes.

Abreha saw that there was no such final sentence. He gave the letter a contemptuous finger flick, rolled it closed with exaggerated disdain, and sealed it deliberately. Telemakos stood breathless, waiting to be told off or struck for the insolence he had committed. He could scarcely believe his bluff had worked, but the letter was sealed.

"Consider yourself fortunate," the najashi commented, his voice expressionless. "The monks on Debra Damo would not afford us pen and parchment, in the sequestered imprisonment that my brothers and I all endured as children, under the tyranny of our uncle Caleb when he was emperor of Aksum." It was almost as if Abreha were talking to himself, he spoke so indirectly to Telemakos. "It was no matter, though, as we had all been taken from our mother so young that we did not remember, and had no need to write to her." Suddenly the najashi looked up. "You still sign yourself Telemakos Meder. What does Meder mean to you?"

The question took him by surprise. "It's my father's name," Telemakos answered.

"It is the Ethiopic name Medraut took when he came to Aksum," Abreha said. "Meder, lord of the land. It is not his real name. Meder is an ancient god of Aksum, abandoned for the Christ two hundred years ago and more. For you, now, it is a name that is . . . inappropriate, and pretentious, as if you were to go about styling yourself after your dead uncle Lleu, the prince of Britain. You must sign yourself Athtar of the sky; the Morningstar, the name given you by your Socotran kinsman, your uncle and master the magus Dawit Alta'ir. You belong to Himyar, now."

"But I haven't yet formally pledged you my service," Telemakos murmured bleakly. He did not want to give up his own name. "And Morningstar was only given to me as a jest."

"You are not yet lord of any land that I know of."

Telemakos stood staring down at the patterned carpet. The silk weave was so thick that the najashi's footsteps had left impressions in it. Telemakos remembered how rough it had felt against his lips when he had knelt against it and begged Abreha's forgiveness, the night he had broken into Abreha's writing desk. Now he found himself wishing that he was on his knees rather than standing upright, so he could hide his face.

The najashi looked up at Telemakos from beneath his heavy frown and repeated coldly:

"You sign yourself Meder, lord of the land, and you boast of your disgrace. Do you count yourself so far above other mortals, my shining one, that you make a jest of the order I carry in my sash, and of the iron nails balanced ready to pierce fast your feet and your single wrist?"

The chimes of the alarm bracelet clicked and clinked as Telemakos flinched.

"I must make a jest of it, or I will be sick," Telemakos said through clenched teeth. "Forgive the jest, my najashi."

"I shall take you to attend an execution, if you are ignorant as to how it is done," Abreha offered quietly.

Even though Telemakos had known a threat was coming—after all, he had more or less asked for it—the najashi's calm menace stopped his heart for a moment.

"*Make an answer,*" the najashi pressed. "*Do you know how it is done?*"

"Sir, I do know," Telemakos whispered. "I do. I saw an execution my first day here." Then he added in a storm of polite, clipped fury, "It was the crucifixion of a pirate in a public square in al-Muza. I came on it by accident. Athena saw it, too; hasn't she mentioned it in all her visits with you? She was only a baby. She dreams about it sometimes, she mutters in her sleep. 'Poor feet. Poor feet.' You have a stronger stomach than I, my najashi, if you care to witness such a spectacle more than once. I would rather take such punishment myself than give the order to deal it out."

Telemakos stopped to draw breath. Abreha, too, said nothing for a moment, almost as though Telemakos's outburst had been a command for silence. Then he asked, frowning but intrigued, "That must have been scant hours before you first came to me. Why didn't you tell me when we met, if it appalled you so?"

"I did not want to poison our first meeting!"

Abreha sat back. He went for so long without speaking that Telemakos felt his initial relief at the sealing of his letter eaten away by evil doubts.

Maybe he has seen through my deceit all along. Maybe he is toying with me.

But the najashi's voice when he spoke next was unexpectedly mild, a voice of gentle fondness and regret.

"How I wish that you were battling at my side, Telemakos Morningstar."

He held himself together up the endless flights and across the scriptorium, but as he came down the short stair that led into the Great Globe Room, he doubled up beneath the crystal stars hanging from the ceiling and vomited over the bottom step. Dawit looked up, unseeing, over the top of the abacus he was mending. His fingers did not stop moving, but he gave a snort of disgust.

"You break or foul everything you touch," the Star Master commented in his usual dry tone. "You are destroying my work-place. Go send for a cloth and a jug of water."

Telemakos wrote a letter to Medraut containing cryptic warnings for Gebre Meskal of the najashi's threat to the Hanish Islands. He could not think of a way to mention the islands by name. He reminded his father of the conversation he had overheard between Medraut and the emperor on the night of the accident that had cost Telemakos his arm, when Medraut had derided the value of the islands. Telemakos's cautious message was so oblique he knew it would be incomprehensible. He sent a similar warning again in a letter to his mother, and read them aloud to Abreha on the same afternoon, one after the other, his stomach churning. Three of the lithe and soulful saluki hounds were curled at the najashi's side; they held their heads alert and watchful, eyeing Telemakos as though they were waiting for the order to run him to ground.

But once again the najashi rolled and sealed the letters without objection.

When he had finished, Abreha stood up and spread his hand across the middle of Telemakos's shoulders to steer him out of his study. The inside of the najashi's heavy signet weighed like lead against the base of Telemakos's neck; it was still warm with the touch of the wax Abreha had used to seal the letters.

Abreha wears Solomon's ring and lives in Solomon's palace, Telemakos thought; Solomon is his ancestor. The najashi rules in Himyar as if by birthright. He styles himself mukarrib, federator, like Himyar's ancient kings. But he is Aksumite, like me. He was not born to his reign here; he was chosen for it. He is the keystone of an alliance of tribes and kingdoms. He is respected, and he is fair, and he has been kind to me.

Telemakos's eyes were burning again.

He glanced back longingly at the salukis as Abreha guided him into the reception chamber. He would have given his soul to call one of these dogs his own. He scarcely ever saw them now that he was forbidden to visit the kennels.

As Telemakos was about to step into the corridor where his guards were waiting for him, Queen Muna came in carrying Athena.

She would not have done it if she had known Telemakos would be there. Athena was nearly two years old, rapidly learning to express herself with equal fluency in South Arabian and Ethiopic, and she kept her loyalties plainly clear.

"*Boy!*" she screamed, lunging toward Telemakos. "*Tena's boy!*" She became a demon whirlwind of wild bronze hair and smooth brown limbs, her gray eyes wide and glittering. When Muna did not let her go, Athena bit her. Muna gasped and put the baby on the floor.

Abreha abandoned ceremony. He gripped Telemakos by the back of his shirt, hauled him through the door, and slammed it shut behind him. Then he let go of Telemakos, and they stood still together for a moment, with the waiting guards, listening to the screeching from inside. They could hear Athena scrabbling at the door, and Muna trying to calm her.

"I'm sorry," the najashi said. "Go."

"Please don't hurt her," Telemakos croaked.

"Don't be stupid, boy. She's here to play with the dogs. You know how she loves them."

Telemakos went back upstairs, bowed to dismiss his guard, and crossed the scriptorium. Harith the librarian gave him a skeptical glance as he passed; two visiting historians did not look up from their work. Telemakos sat down with his head against his knees on the bottom step of the Globe Room.

"Do you need the basin?" Dawit inquired warily.

"I'm all right." Telemakos swallowed, and swallowed again, despairing of the long season that stretched ahead of him.

II

SUNBIRD IN A CAGE

THE WORST OF the daily march to and from the training ground was passing the door to the children's room. Behind this door, or through it if it were open, came sounds that reminded Telemakos of what he was missing. Sometimes, the tame songbirds trilled and fluted; the Scions, Abreha's royal foster children, who would inherit most of Himyar's kingdoms, sang together to Queen Muna's lyre; or the increasingly unmanageable Athena screamed in hysterical fury or threw things across the room.

Abreha did not arm Telemakos's jailers with anything more dangerous than whips. The najashi rotated the watchmen daily, and they were all chosen from his personal guard; they took their orders seriously and were not to be won over by charm or familiarity, or by superstitious fear of Telemakos's British eyes, steely and strange as witchcraft in an Aksumite face. These men made it clear that playing nursemaid to a disobedient boy was beneath their station, whatever he was and whatever his crime. They tolerated no childishness in Telemakos, treating him almost as a disgraced equal.

One morning Telemakos boldly defied his escort on his way back up the stairs, and turned out of the corridor and through the door into the children's room.

"Out," ordered one of the guards.

Telemakos paid no attention. They had to follow him into the room, ducking around the hanging birdcages of willow and silver. Twelve of Abreha's fourteen royal foster children looked up from their breakfast in surprise. Only Athena and the two youngest Scions, Habib and Lu'lu, were missing; they were presumably in the nursery with Queen Muna.

"Come away now," the watchman told Telemakos. "Don't shame yourself before your fellows."

Telemakos made his way purposefully toward the nursery, and the other guard cracked his whip around Telemakos's ankles. The sting made him miss his step; his legs were bare beneath his sandal straps. He stopped, not because he was afraid of the whip, but because it was embarrassing. The Royal Scions were all staring.

"Turn and face me," the soldier ordered. He spoke as calmly as if he were offering Telemakos a second helping of rice. Telemakos hesitated, then confronted his escort squarely.

He saw, as he turned, that the three eldest of the Scions no longer showed any interest in this scene. Tall Jibril, motherly

Inas, and the dark, edgy young king Shadi had all bent low over their bowls of honey yogurt.

"Will you stand fast to be disciplined?" the soldier with the whip asked Telemakos. "Or must Butrus hold you still?"

"I'll stand," Telemakos said.

The soldier struck him in the face with the tail of his lash, sharply and accurately. It left a narrow, burning blaze across his cheek.

"You are required to do as you are bid," the soldier told him, with the same sure, controlled lack of excitement. "If anyone asks how you came by that mark on your face, you are to tell them you were whipped for disobedience. Now leave this hall and continue up the stairs to the scriptorium, where the Star Master waits to give you your daily instruction."

Telemakos, his face afire more with humiliation than anything else, stalked back out to the corridor and continued up the stairs.

"What is that?" Harith the librarian in the scriptorium asked, when he came to the landing to let Telemakos through to the Great Globe Room. He stabbed a short finger toward Telemakos's cheek, pointing. The soldiers stood waiting and listening, and Telemakos knew he could not lie.

"It's a lash mark."

"What were you lashed for?"

Telemakos bit his lip. He was beginning to realize how this particular punishment was supposed to work.

"Disobedience," he managed to answer, through clenched teeth.

Harith escorted him to Dawit, who was waiting at the door to the Globe Room. "Your apprentice has got a great red burn across his face," the librarian told him conversationally.

The Star Master's cataracts so blinded him that he would never have noticed, but he knew the ritual.

"Oh? How intriguing." Dawit's tone was as dry as always. "Tell me what's happened to your face, boy."

"*I was whipped for disobedience,*" Telemakos snarled.

"You need not growl at me, or I shall ask them to whip you for insolence as well," Dawit said mildly. "Come and set out the charcoal drawing sticks. I have a new project I want you to begin."

That was all Dawit ever said about it. But it was ten days before the bruise faded, and Telemakos was forced to explain it over and over: to Queen Muna's haughty handmaid Rasha, to the attendants who brought his meals up to him, indeed, to anyone who came into the library. Gedar the olive merchant, who was Aksumite himself and a neighbor of Telemakos's grandfather, spent long, self-important hours explaining his inventories to the najashi's librarian, and he always looked up if Telemakos passed. He spoke with utterly false concern. "Your whip weal has nearly gone, young prince, Lij Telemakos. It will stop embarrassing you soon enough. Haven't you become well behaved, though!"

Telemakos had already sent his aunt a coded message denouncing Gedar's deep involvement in the najashi's conspiracy against the Aksumite emperor. It was worse than being lashed to have to be polite to Gedar.

There was also Tharan to face, Abreha's lieutenant, who directed Telemakos and the najashi's youthful soldiers in their spear throwing. The cadets themselves were relentless.

"You've still got that mark on your face, Aksumite. Tell us again, where did that come from?" They badgered him every morning for ten days. And afterward, as well, they would occasionally remind him: "Hey, Aksumite, didn't you used to have a red mark on your face? How did you come by that?"

The young spearmen ribbed him equally without mercy over the alarm bracelet the najashi made him wear as part of his ongoing punishment for eavesdropping. Every cast Telemakos threw was accompanied by a flourish of silver bells.

Telemakos detested the alarm. More than anything he hated its gaudiness. It consisted of a narrow silver band fixed snugly just above his elbow, so thickly hung about with filigreed bells and wire tassels that it shivered musically if Telemakos so much as coughed. He had always been able to move with the sure stealth of a leopard stalking its prey, and the perpetual tattling of the charms maddened him. The noise kept him awake, and the bracelet itched. He had tried persistently to work it off in the early days of wearing it; but it was nearly two years since he had lost his left arm to blood poisoning, and his right elbow was impossible to reach with anything more practical than his toes. He could not shift the bracelet.

"Is that a trophy, or a love knot?" the young warriors teased. "Which queenlet has made a favorite of you?"

"Maybe the Aksumite thinks he belongs in Afar," one of them suggested.

Afar—

This took him utterly off guard.

Telemakos missed the next throw by so far his lance did not even strike the butt. *The sunbird is flying to Afar—* How could any of them possibly know?

Telemakos picked up another spear, without altering his line of sight, trying to hide how much the remark had jarred him.

It was three years, three years since he had been imprisoned at the Afar salt mines in the Aksumite desert, spying out smugglers for Gebre Meskal. It haunted him at random, triggered by a smell or a touch, and still, for a moment, he was there. Blindfolded, his arms fixed firmly at his sides with leather cord, he stood feigning deafness and trying not to quake as Anako, the governor of Deire, debated aloud how best to blind him permanently. It was a nightmare that swallowed him whole, even when he was fully awake. It might happen if he vainly tried to catch his balance with his lost arm, or if the wind lifted a fold of his shamma shawl over his face by accident, or at the smell of baboon or a certain combination of sweat and dust. The touch of salt against his lips or fingertips sometimes seemed to burn like flame. The sunbird in Afar! If Abreha should ever know—

Telemakos's deception there had brought about the destruction of Abreha's black market in salt. No man alive should ever know. So how on earth could Abreha's young spearmen know?

After a moment the innocence of the jeer came to him. The Afar warriors wore bracelets to tally the men they had killed. They also wore more sinister decorations, Telemakos recalled, cut from their victims' bodies.

He threw again. The dratted bells shook merrily at his elbow.

"If I were an Afar tribesman, which I am not, I would wear ornaments that were a deal more fascinating than this." Telemakos made a rude and vicious gesture, and to his surprise and delight he got a good laugh out of his companions.

"Enough!" Tharan barked.

Telemakos endured the scoffing. He was deeply grateful that he had not been pulled straight out of training and forbidden ever to touch a spear again. If there was any consolation to be dragged from the wreckage of his standing in Abreha's court, it was that he might one day be allowed to hunt again with the najashi and his beautiful saluki hounds.

Athena treated the queen Muna with savage dislike. She would not let Muna touch her, and had to be cleaned and dressed by Muna's attendant Rasha and a team of maidservants. Athena stripped the leaves from every tree and vine on the terrace as high as she could reach. She threw a bowl through one of the jeweled windows. She fouled her bed and smeared the mess across the walls in the morning before anyone was awake. In desperation, Muna's women began to tie Athena down at night. And then she would scream in fury until she could no longer stay awake, and go on sobbing sporadically even in her sleep. Telemakos dreaded the day it might occur to them to drug her. Muna was allowed access to the medicines, Telemakos knew, because it was she who distributed the painkilling powders he was offered if his ruined shoulder hurt him. Telemakos quietly scorned opium, but Athena might not have a choice.

Telemakos overheard Muna weeping, too, confiding in her servant Rasha, who had been her companion since childhood.

"Whatever that boy has done," the queen sobbed, "is it worth my husband punishing all the household? Have I not been punished already for my own sins? I am second wife to my husband, second mother to these motherless children, never beloved as the first. It is true I have been faithless, but is it not enough I must bear the loss of my own children to plague, that I must also endure this mockery of motherhood?"

Telemakos bit his knuckles as he stared down at one of the fine maps the British ambassador had left behind when he had suddenly gone home, two weeks before Telemakos arrived in San'a. Gwalchmei of the Orcades had brought the British maps to Himyar intending to send them on to his cousin Goewin in

Aksum, but the plague quarantine had stopped their onward journey. Now Abreha wanted copies made for his own library before the maps went to Aksum.

Telemakos loved these British maps. They had been made by Goewin's mother, Ginevra, for her husband, Artos, the high king. It enchanted Telemakos to see and touch things his grandfather had seen and touched, four thousand miles away, twenty years and how many battles ago. Artos the high king of Britain had studied these, made notes on them in his own hand, amended them. Now they lay safe on another drafting table, for Telemakos to read. And he was Artos's grandson.

The almost irresistible temptation to alter the maps before they went to Goewin, to try to conceal some message in them, drove Telemakos to study them so carefully that he was on the verge of being able to reproduce them from memory. He dreamed about them. He could look beyond the painted lines and see the winding rivers, wider and deeper than any he had ever known, never dry. An image of Hadrian's Wall, the mortal remains of Rome in Britain, took shape in his mind as he stared at its long path from coast to coast across the island. It seemed to him he could picture it clearly: a vast ridge of rock and earth, stretching ruinous through miles of barren, foreign moor and forest. But there was no one who could tell him what it really looked like. It was the better part of a year since the British ambassador Gwalchmei had left Himyar.

I want to make a map that Dawit can read himself, Telemakos thought. Even if it doesn't carry any secret meaning. If the magus could read the maps I made, Abreha wouldn't have to check them. I should like to be able to do something that doesn't make me feel as if the najashi is always breathing down my neck.

"Morningstar?"

Now all the palace used the name Dawit had given Telemakos in ridicule of his bright hair.

"Morningstar!"

The sound came from below, a hissed whisper. Inas of Ma'in, eldest of Abreha's foster daughters, stood in the nursery directly beneath the pulley hole cut in the floor of the Great Globe Room. She was looking up. When Telemakos peered down, they were gazing at each other face-to-face, less than two yards between them. Inas had dark brown eyes and thick black hair, and the skin of her oval face was lighter than his own; the people of the Himyar highlands were generally not as dark as the Aksumites. The scratches Athena had torn in Inas's cheeks had scabbed over. Her face looked dreadful. Telemakos hoped she would not carry permanent marks.

"You're alone?" Inas's voice was urgent.

Telemakos blinked at her, the Himyar children's silent affirmation.

"We thought you would be alone. Queen Muna said she had to take her father, the Star Master, marketing for more paints, since you're not allowed out to do it for him, and he doesn't trust anyone else."

"You will be in trouble if you're caught talking to me," Telemakos rasped back.

Inas spoke low and quickly.

"Not much. Anyone caught talking to you will be shut up without food for a day. But you'll be whipped again, properly, outside at the posts, like a servant."

"Never believe it," Telemakos scoffed. "They wouldn't dare beat me on purpose. Everyone has babied me since I lost my arm. If I take a fall riding, or if I get struck in mock combat when we use the unbarbed staves, they always make a great fuss afterward with salves and painkillers." These were given to him at the written instruction of Telemakos's physician father, and paid for by the emperor of Aksum himself, whose pet lion had tried to chew off Telemakos's arm. Telemakos had grown tired of refusing opium. He took the portions given him and then disposed of them, unused, in the hidden pouch at the back of Athena's carrying saddle.

"The najashi won't whip me," Telemakos added, to pacify Inas, though his confidence in this was hollow.

"He will. They will give you opium afterward, in deference to your father's wishes, but they will not spare you the indignity. Do you see? Any one of us can have you lashed, just by calling out your name, and all we will pay for it will be a day's solitude."

She paused, suddenly, and Telemakos waited, staring down at her torn face, wondering why she was bothering to tell him this when she could instead so easily use it against him.

"We wanted you to know. If you pass us in the corridors we won't look at you. We all agreed; even the little ones understand. We will act as though we do not know you, but it's not because we despise you, do you see? It's because we don't want you to be whipped."

She gazed up at him, waiting for an answer.

Telemakos glanced over his shoulder toward the open door that led to the scriptorium, wondering where the librarian was. Harith could be pettily vindictive; he did not like the traffic that the children made through his formerly silent alabaster-roofed hall, since the Star Master had acquired an apprentice who had let his baby sister use the lapis ink blocks as finger paints.

Telemakos looked down through the floor again. Inas was still waiting below, her expression anxious.

"Is your face all right?" he asked.

"My face? Oh, Athena's scratches. It's nothing. They're not deep—she's only got baby nails. Little monster, she's so sad; I wish she'd let me hold her. But she only wants you. 'Boy, boy, where is Tena's boy,' she cries, every waking minute."

"Where is she now?"

"The najashi took her down to see the pet lion. And that creature Menelik is an emotional beast as well, as starving for your attention as your sister! The najashi is still trying to teach him to hunt like a dog, do you know?"

"Yes, he tells me all about his hunting," Telemakos whispered. "The lion hasn't caught anything yet."

"The kennelmen don't like to run it loose without you

there. It's not so obedient for the najashi as it is for you." Inas took a deep breath. Then she added quickly, "If you want to send a letter to your mother without the najashi reading it, drop it through the ceiling here when there's one of us below. If it's safe we'll bang the shutters three times, and if there's no one else in the Globe Room, you can send a letter down."

If he did that, and any of the fourteen Scions reported it or was caught, by the terms of his covenant with Abreha, Telemakos could be crucified.

"I won't," he whispered. "I won't. It's a noble offer, Inas, but I don't want you to be punished with me. Thank you for the offer." His throat suddenly ached. "Thank you."

"We are with you," she said. "We are all with you."

With that she smiled at him suddenly, then stepped outside his limited view of the room below. He did not dare call out to see if she was still there.

Telemakos swallowed the ache in the back of his throat and sat down again to the map spread over the Star Master's writing table. But now, after Inas's hurried vow of secret faith, the names of the rivers and cities ran together in his sight as though he had spilled a pot of ink across them. He dared not change a single pen stroke on these irrelevant documents; Abreha would check them against the copies. Mother of God, Telemakos thought, why am I learning this? What does any of it matter? Why would I ever need to know what water courses run near Hadrian's Wall?

And still he had not warned Gebre Meskal of the najashi's threat to the Hanish Islands.

That night Telemakos dreamed he was walking on Hadrian's Wall. His left arm was sound and whole again, which made his heart sink, for in the back of his mind he knew that invariably some person or creature would hack it off before the dream ended. The mist came down so low he could not see his feet. Coming toward him along the wall in the opposite direction were two shapeless figures, one taller than the other, both black against the gray of the lowering sky. Telemakos knew that one was Gedar. The other he thought must be Anako, the man the salt smugglers called the Lazarus, who had first tried to blind Telemakos and then tried to kill him: the man Telemakos had sentenced to exile. They would have to pass close to each other, for the wall was narrow. Telemakos dreaded that his grandfather's neighbor would greet him by name and let Anako know who he was. He kept his head down and did not look, but Gedar caught him by the wrist as they came abreast of each other.

"Morningstar," Gedar sneered, but that was not a name Anako knew, so Telemakos was still safe. He dared not protest or struggle. The merchant's hand burned like cold fire where it was locked around Telemakos's wrist, like the icy touch of hailstones, until he could no longer feel his arm.

"So at last you've told your emperor all the najashi's plans for stealing his island fortress. What king would trust you now?"

Gedar taunted. "Liar. Deceiver. Traitorous toad. You should be named serpent, not sunbird."

But it was not Gedar's voice. It was Medraut's voice, low and dark and full of music. Telemakos knew he had mistaken both men. It was his father condemning him so poisonously, and the other man was Medraut's dead brother, Lleu, the prince of Britain, dark-haired and white-faced and imperious. They were allied against him. Telemakos tried to pull free of the cold hand that gripped his wrist; his dead arm came away in his father's hand. Telemakos fled back the way he had come, stumbling, all out of balance over the old stones of the wall he could not see in the mist around his feet.

III

ADVICE TO THE NAJASHI

THOUGH HALF HIS letters home were truly innocent of any intrigue, Telemakos felt he had to construct pitfalls for himself, to keep him on his guard, in case he should alert Abreha to his change of mood when he was not endangering himself. He took to baiting the najashi.

> There are many empty rooms in the Ghumdan palaces.
> The najashi likes to play mother to the small orphans.
> His spearmen are not so well trained as Gebre Meskal's.

Telemakos included this last comment in a letter to his grandfather. He meant nothing more artful by it than to nettle Abreha with its scornful tone. When he read it aloud, the najashi stopped Telemakos short and ordered, "Repeat that."

Telemakos did, and felt himself go cold as he realized how much it sounded like a general's report.

"And again," Abreha ordered quietly.

Halfway through his third reading of it, Telemakos faltered, the flattened palm frond trembling so in his grip that he could not make out the writing on it. He went down on his knees with a jangle of silver and bowed his head.

Abreha's signet ring brushed cool and rough against the base of Telemakos's skull as the najashi laid his hand over the back of his neck.

"Hush, child." Abreha spoke soothingly. "To send plainly stated military information to the imperial parliament of Aksum would be a fool's mistake, and you are no fool. Destroy this letter, and write another."

Telemakos rewrote it sitting at Abreha's own desk, beneath the najashi's watchful, frowning glare, and gave away no hint of the iron menace that shadowed him except in that his shaking pen produced writing that was more unreadable than usual.

He was careful not to mention Abreha's soldiers again. He had still the threatened Hanish Islands to tell of, and that was a deal more dangerous to mention than the palace guard. He began to look forward to the time when Aksum's highland roads would be closed by the Long Rains, and he would have a reasonable excuse not to write home. He was rarely allowed a moment's idleness anyway, and the scheming was beginning to exhaust him.

Dawit, sadistically, liked best to set his apprentice several tasks at once. Telemakos would have to polish the enormous teak-and-crystal compass from Cathay, translate a Greek geography aloud into South Arabian, and calculate latitudes on an abacus all at the same time. He was awkward and self-conscious, juggling scrolls and pens and tools with his single hand. The pens had been Athena's province; she had sorted and cleaned them and passed them out. Telemakos missed her there to pick up the things he dropped and to hold his pages flat.

While Telemakos drew, the Star Master plied him with endless mental arithmetical calculations or drilled him in lists of stars or rivers or the principal cities of Persia.

"Name the tribal kingdoms of Himyar and southern Arabia."

"Kinda and Qataban, Hadramawt, Awsan—" Telemakos hesitated. Through the pulley hole came a noise of torrential weeping, but for once it was not Athena. This was one of the bigger girls. Inas?

"Ma'in." Telemakos hesitated again. He bent over the map he was drawing, trying to recite the required list of kingdoms mechanically but concentrating on the voice below. It was not Inas of Ma'in. It was Malika, the lovely, preening girl who called herself queen of Sheba. Her wordless keening alternated with angry, sobbed protests.

"Sheba," Telemakos added.

With the side of his hand Dawit pretended to slash his own throat, commanding instant silence. He put the other hand behind his ear in exaggerated parody of a careful listener.

Telemakos laid down his pen and bent his head. "I am forbidden to eavesdrop in this palace," he said evenly, straining to catch the sense of the outburst below.

"Pish. You are not eavesdropping; even Harith at the other end of the scriptorium can hear that. Their racket would wake the dead. Come and listen."

Dawit knelt with his head tilted low over the pulley hole; his beard hung down the shaft. No one in the room below seemed to notice him at all.

Malika was wailing. "I shall not, it was my mother's palace and I shall not dower it to a warrior lordling with no wealth of his own. I do not care how famed he is in battle, I am a queen, not a prize!"

Inas's calm, firm voice said soothingly, "Of course you are queen. Be heroic! Don't you see, if you marry a man of petty title, your kingdom remains intact, your own?"

"It does not," Malika sobbed. "It all belongs to him."

There was another spate of speechless weeping, and then Queen Muna's soft voice murmured something comforting that Telemakos did not catch. He glanced at Dawit. The old man was watching him, or trying to, through eyes like needle slits. The Star Master whispered, rather loudly, "All the girls go running to my daughter when they feel sorry for themselves. They are down there wiping one another's eyes, cuddling and kissing like kittens in a basket."

Muna's voice floated aloft, then, more clearly: "But you know, my love, it will belong to your husband, whoever it is you marry. Socotra is only mine by wedlock, though I was born there."

"I should make a *union*. Not a trophy," Malika said bitterly.

Telemakos had never heard her say anything so profoundly serious. Then she ruined it by adding, with deep petulance, "And I want someone younger and prettier."

"What's her age?" Telemakos whispered.

"She's ten," Dawit answered. "It is only a betrothal. Nothing will happen for some years yet. You see why the najashi is breaking the news early! She'll have time to get used to the idea."

Gedar the despicable olive merchant went back to Aksum before the Long Rains began there. He made a special trip up to the scriptorium to ask Telemakos, with oily goodwill, if there was any token he could bear home with him for the lady Turunesh Kidane. Telemakos spent a furious, sickening afternoon composing an appropriate letter to his mother for Gedar to carry.

Arrest Gedar, Telemakos wrote.

"Dearest Mother, I miss you so much," he read aloud for Abreha. "Give my love to all, my father, and Grandfather, and my aunt. I am still kept apart from Athena, and miss her as much as I miss you; still I watch for her daily, wishing I could just once follow her when she appears. I have only seen Athena a single time this week, but I watch for her always.

"She isn't bearing our separation well. They can't let her near the songbirds; she tries to fling them out the windows. I have seen Athena arrest Lu'lu, the youngest of Abreha's children, and bite her on the hand like a nasty little dog. She treats Queen Muna with such contempt it embarrasses me. Why does my lady endure it? Muna adores Athena. Gedar and the magus and the najashi's children have all stopped trying to make her be nice to them, but Muna never even complains. My heart bleeds for the abuse she takes so selflessly on behalf of the unfeeling little wretch."

The charms were tinking softly. Telemakos pressed the bracelet against his ribs to steady the quaking. He thought: I am going to learn to keep this blasted alarm quiet. That will be a good challenge.

There were two more paragraphs of this drivel still to read. He had woven the message in three times: *Arrest Gedar. Arrest Gedar. Arrest Gedar.*

Abreha listened absently, gazing down at the outline of Britain that Telemakos had sketched on a sheet of fine linen. It was the beginning of his idea to make a store of maps that Dawit would be able to follow with his fingertips. Telemakos read to the end of the letter, and the najashi held out his hand without looking up. Telemakos passed the strip over for it to be sealed.

"What misery there is throughout my house," Abreha said quietly. Telemakos stood watching through his lowered lashes while the najashi, frowning forbiddingly, pressed the star-and-lion sigil of Solomon into the hot wax.

"You are right to observe that my queen suffers her ills without complaint," Abreha said. "I wonder that she doesn't confide in her father."

Telemakos said nothing.

"Or in Rasha, her lady-in-waiting?" Abreha prompted.

Telemakos sucked in a sharp breath. "You have put me under pain of death as a suspected spy," he said in a low voice. "If I overheard such a complaint, and I spoke of it, would I not risk being dragged down to the Street of Shade for execution?"

"I fear I have made you overcautious," the najashi said. He blew on his signet ring in the warming pan, to cool it. "And in truth, I do not need you to tell me that my queen is unhappy."

The najashi gazed down at the linen map that covered his desk. "I can make your sister eat when she refuses food from anyone else but you," Abreha murmured. "I can make her lie quiet in my arms until she falls asleep, even though she has spent the past hour screaming herself hoarse. But I cannot make her love my queen. She is too little to understand. She blames Muna, not me, for sending you away from her."

He fell silent again. Perhaps he was lost in his study of the map that lay before him. But it seemed as though he were waiting for an answer, or a suggestion, from Telemakos.

"When I was a deal younger, if ever I drove my mother to despair, my father would take her riding," Telemakos hazarded; "the two of them alone together."

This had actually happened, once. It was memorable.

"You are a consummate tactician, Morningstar," said Abreha. "That's what the poet Tarafa says, as well. 'When grief assails me, straightway I ride it off.' I shall consider your domestic advice." He looked up at Telemakos at last. "We will send this map of yours off to the seamstresses to embroider. Your instructions are clear enough as to where to fix the beads and sequins. I shall ask them to give you a bolt of cloth for your own use, so you may complete this series, and if Dawit is satisfied that you know what you're doing, then you need not send the rest of them to me to check. What made you think of this? Such a simple idea, really, to make the lines visible to the fingertips as well as to the eye."

"My grandfather Artos had something like it hanging in his study. Goewin told me about it. It was a floor plan of his house that his wife Ginevra made for him. She made all his maps."

"How precise you are," the najashi said, glancing back down at the faint lines of charcoal on the linen sheet. "Telemakos Draftsman, we should call you. I admired Artos your grandfather deeply, Morningstar. Your father called him 'the engineer king.' Artos rebuilt every ruin he came across, wall and palace and aqueduct, all throughout his kingdom. It was his work that inspired me to restore the great dam at Marib. I will take you to see it, someday."

Telemakos considered, and dared a small challenge. "Will you?"

"I promise you," Abreha answered seriously, gazing up at him again with his faint frown and sad black eyes. "Next year, perhaps, when the lion has learned to hunt. We will take it up to Marib. In the meantime I will have Dawit teach you the complexities of the irrigation systems that water this dry land and keep it green, so you can make sense of what you are seeing."

Telemakos was bewildered by this promise; he did not know what he had done to deserve it.

"Why, my najashi?" he asked.

"Because your aunt obliges me to see that you learn such things as part of your apprenticeship," Abreha answered dryly. He rolled the map carefully shut, moved Telemakos's duplicitous sealed letter to one side, and folded his hands together on the writing table. He gazed up at Telemakos expectantly.

"Tell me what you are thinking," Abreha commanded.

Telemakos stared for a moment at the letter he had written and thought, *Arrest Gedar.*

"When are you going to get a new British ambassador?" he asked.

"When Constantine the high king sends me one. And your aunt must give her approval, as well. You know how long it takes for messages to come and go from Britain." The najashi laughed. "I have you, in the meantime. You are half-British. I am sure you have advice for me. How can I strengthen my kingdom?"

Telemakos hesitated, wondering where this banter was meant to lead him. He did not want to talk about Himyar's strengths or weaknesses; mapping distant Britain was a much safer topic. Then he remembered Inas's pledge of loyalty.

"You should make unions among the Royal Scions," Telemakos said. "Let Malika and Shadi wed, when they come of age. They are both devoted to you, and their marriage will unite Sheba and Qataban. It won't increase anyone's name or title, nor expand your dominion, but it will keep it sound."

"I shall put that suggestion before my Federation!" Abreha exclaimed.

Telemakos protested carefully, "My najashi, I think you mock me."

"On the contrary. Let me grant you a petition in exchange for such good advice. What grace would you ask of the king of Himyar?"

Telemakos did not, now, believe Abreha to be trifling with him. He sensed that the najashi was testing him in some unknown way, as Gebre Meskal had done on several occasions, and though he did not know the reason for this test, he thought he could direct it toward some neutral good and make return for a forgotten favor. Telemakos remembered the day he arrived in Himyar, and the stranger who had come to his aid and stood by him with unnecessary loyalty.

He said hesitantly, "Do you remember, my najashi, how I told you I had seen an execution in al-Muza, on my first day in Himyar?"

Abreha said nothing. Telemakos finally dared to raise his eyes from the floor to the najashi's face, and Abreha blinked his silent permission to continue. His face was unreadable. Telemakos quickly looked at his feet again.

"I had a guide in al-Muza that day, a boy near my own age, the nephew of a tailor called Laban," Telemakos said. "His name was Iskinder. He told me his ambition was to join al-Muza's city guard, and though he was bold and strong and honorable, he thought he wouldn't be accepted in the guard because he had no one to recommend him. I would dare beg your endorsement of Iskinder as your soldier, if you could do that."

"Of all things, why should you think to ask this?"

The answer that tried to force its way aloud between his teeth could not be spoken. *Because, my najashi, someone has to carry out your executions, and Iskinder is willing to do it.*

But he managed to answer politely. "Because it's easily granted, and something you are likely to grant," Telemakos said frankly, "and if you do, we can both be content to think ourselves virtuous and generous."

"Is it right that you should volunteer another to pledge me his service, when you withhold your own?"

"Sir!" Telemakos protested. "You yourself asked me to withhold my pledge until you had trained me to use a spear. But that was before you placed me under suspicion as a spy. Would you trust my pledge now?"

"Perhaps not," Abreha said. "Perhaps not. You are forthright enough in declaring your loyalty to my cousin the Aksumite emperor."

Not enough, Telemakos thought. I have not been forthright enough. Gebre Meskal does not know the danger that awaits him in Hanish.

The najashi paused, then said again, "And yet I pray that one day you will battle at my side, Telemakos Morningstar."

IV

SEASON OF STARS

GEDAR WAS NO longer in San'a now, but Telemakos had made so much incidental mention of the oil merchant's name in his coded letters that he felt obliged to mention him in innocence as well. He sent a letter to his father describing last season's hunt with the lion Menelik. Gedar had been there as an observer. It was old news, but it was easy to bring up naturally, because Abreha was generous in discussing the lion's training with Telemakos. It was like a flaw in the najashi's forbidding nature, how eagerly he looked forward to taking Telemakos hunting with the lion again.

Telemakos wrote to Medraut:

You would think it sheer lunacy, this experiment of teaching a lion to hunt like a dog. This lion is not as fast as the wonderful salukis, and much more stubborn. Lions hunt naturally in stealth, by night, creeping up on prey and tak-

ing it in a burst of sudden strength; and most of their hunt-
ing is down to the females, in any case. Menelik will look
like a big black termite mound creeping through the grass,
once his mane starts to grow, and scare everything away.

Abreha gave a brief snort of amusement. "I had not thought of that. You do make me look a fool."

"Shall I paint out this story?" Telemakos offered in bland politeness, his eyes on the floor. He enjoyed needling Abreha about the lion, their one shared interest where Telemakos was on safe footing and certain in his superior knowledge.

"That would not be right," Abreha answered mildly. "Your father is wise enough to draw his own conclusions. Read on."

Abreha can use Menelik now, if need be, to make the killing
blow once the dogs have brought down their prey. But then
Menelik always thinks the kill belongs to him. Abreha may
reason with him at such times, but the lion snaps at all the
others as though they are his cubs, or his mates, and are trying
to cheat him of his masterly share. I hope when my seclusion
is through, Menelik will remember me, because the najashi
estimates that at one year old Menelik weighs as much as a
grown man, and though I, too, have begun rapidly increasing
in stature, I do not think I will catch up to the lion.

The najashi skimmed through the letter himself, as he always did, then sealed it without fuss.

"Can you imagine what your father will make of my lunacy when he reads this tale, Morningstar?" he commented. "Don't be surprised if he forbids you to hunt with me, or orders another long confinement for yourself."

It would be worth it, Telemakos thought, to know that my letters are going where they are supposed to.

He never received any response from his father. He never received anything from Goewin. But it could have meant Abreha was keeping his mail from him. The najashi had done that before; his family's letters made mention of some impenetrable circumstance the najashi did not want Telemakos to discover, perhaps to do with the departed British ambassador. The letters arriving from Telemakos's mother were two months old, and predated his disgrace.

Endless weeks passed. It was nearly a year since Telemakos had first arrived in Himyar. The apricots were harvested, Athena passed her second birthday, and lordlings from all Arabia began gathering for the Great Assembly, the yearly meeting of Abreha's Federation. Telemakos did not witness any of these things. He knew they were happening, or he heard about them from Dawit. He memorized maps and watched the stars and slept on the floor of the Great Globe Room with his head close to the pulley hole, where he could catch the faint breath of Athena's sandalwood-scented hair and hear her self-pitying baby sobs as she cried herself to sleep.

Dawit woke him in the middle of one night, kicking him

gently. It took Telemakos some time to work out that this was real, and not some new abuse of his own dreams.

"Get up, boy," the Star Master barked. "Fetch clean tablets and an abacus, and give them to me to carry. You go ahead, up to the gallery on the roof. The librarian says there's a star shower on."

Telemakos, struggling from sleep, obeyed numbly. He had got used to navigating the Globe Room in the dark, for Dawit rarely bothered to light a lamp in the evening, and Telemakos still could not master the striking of a flint one-handed to make a light himself. Groping in the gloom, Telemakos found three writing tablets fresh with new wax, and a portable abacus with its own stand. Dawit took the things and pushed Telemakos up the steps that led to the door to the scriptorium.

"Go on, go! We're missing it! Harith doesn't know what he's looking at. Every time a star falls he thinks the world is coming to an end. And anyway, he can't count."

Telemakos felt his way along the scriptorium shelves to the narrow stairway that led to the roof. Dawit followed behind, his arms full.

The parapet around the base of the Globe Room's dome was the highest point of the Ghumdan palaces that could be reached without scaling the slopes of the dome itself. There was scarcely room for two men to pass abreast on this terrace, and the stair that led to it was so narrow and steep that you had to climb it face-to both up and down, like a ladder. Telemakos emerged blinking from the black pit of the stairwell to a warm summer night lit faintly by a sliver of new moon, about to set, and streaked silver above and behind him with falling stars.

He could see the silhouettes of half a dozen men leaning against the dome or the rails of the terrace, and realized suddenly that he had not got dressed. He stood limned with starlight, all strengths and flaws on full view to any whose eyes had adjusted enough to the dark to be able to see him.

"Get out of the way," Dawit said behind him, gruffly.

Telemakos stepped aside and crouched low on the parapet, partly out of embarrassment and partly because he was blocking the view. He moved quickly, and the silver bells at his elbow thrashed and jangled like an accompaniment to the strange show in the sky.

"Welcome, young prince," said the najashi's voice. He spoke in Greek, the common language of the Red Sea.

It was impossible to tell which of the figures was Abreha until the najashi made his way along the terrace to meet him. Abreha took off his own short surcoat and slung the heavy embroidered silk over Telemakos's shoulders. Then he offered Telemakos his hand and raised him to his feet.

"Come and join us! I've saved a good place for you, so you may act as Dawit's eyes." The watchers made room for Telemakos deferentially, with good nature. "Come along, stand here. There is room for your abacus by the railing. Dawit, my Star Master, here is a seat for you."

The najashi's robe was too broad for Telemakos. Its folds

flapped loose and got in his way as he tried to erect the abacus, which he just managed to discreetly save from being knocked over the edge of the terrace. He slipped his sound arm free of the trailing sleeve and let the silk hang precariously from one shoulder, hiding the bare stump of his lost arm. The chimes at his elbow shivered and sang.

"Let me muffle those bells," said the najashi, untying his own fine sash. "Their ringing will distract us."

He took Telemakos by the wrist and wrapped the belt of silk again and again around the charm bracelet, tying it off securely. Telemakos watched him do it, aware of the shooting stars littering the sky above him.

"Some princess's sweetheart, is he, your young astrono-mer, wearing her gift as a decoration?" jested a man who spoke Greek with a Persian accent.

"He is adored by his infant sister," Abreha answered lightly. "Little bells keep her entertained. He does not wear them idly, though the right to display some decoration would be his if he were given to vanity. This is Lij Bitwoded Telemakos, the be-loved young prince Telemakos, heir to the Aksumite house of Nebir and a favorite of the emperor Gebre Meskal."

The dark, faceless figures around him bent their heads in respect, there being no room to kneel.

Telemakos stood frozen and astonished, not knowing what to make of this formal introduction.

"Telemakos is apprentice to my cartographer and astronomer,

Dawit Alta'ir. We call him Athtar because it is an ancient name for the Morningstar. Eosphorus, in Greek. Lij Bitwoded Telemakos Eosphorus!"

They laughed spontaneously, and one of them clapped. Abreha laughed also. His laughter was light and merry, like a child's; in the dark it was almost impossible to believe how stern a face he always wore. "You mustn't be offended that we laugh. Your silver hair is luminous as the starlight, and we have been sitting here worrying over too many falling stars. It is a blessed relief to all of us to look on one just rising.

"These men are of the Ashar and Farasan tribes, here for the Great Assembly of my Federation," Abreha contin-ued. "And Julian is a legate from Roman Byzantium, here to observe the Assembly. You're fluent in Latin, Morningstar, half-British as you are? You must translate for Julian. You may serve as his cupbearer during the Assembly and feast, and see that he understands all the talk. He was in Britain many years ago, as legate there when Artos was alive."

"Thank you, my najashi," Telemakos murmured.

"Go on, begin your calculations."

Telemakos stared at the ethereal sky, frowning, and began mechanically passing beads across the wires of the abacus. He had forgotten what it felt like, what it sounded like, to be able to move without making a noise. He held the beads still for a minute and savored the quiet before he began to count aloud for Dawit Alta'ir.

"Two at once, just then, the trails lasting five seconds. One with a long track of twenty degrees of sky, and the other bursting like a fireball at the end of its track . . ."

He stared overhead, waiting for the next. Gebre Meskal's astronomer had also been in the habit of counting random falling stars, fewer and fewer every year since Telemakos became his student. Telemakos, born of a generation too young to remember the quiet skies before the great comet of ten years ago, did not find starfire ominous, but the other watchers had fallen silent as Telemakos spoke. Their silence made him feel self-conscious, as though he were undergoing a formal examination, or a trial.

But it was such a blessed relief to have the jangling charms stopped.

"One yellow track, one silver . . ." For a long time there was no sound but his own voice cataloguing the shooting stars, the slip of bead and wire as he tallied the streaks and flashes, and the scratch of Dawit's stylus in the wax. Telemakos could even hear the faint dripping of the water clock as it counted out the passing hours. Every now and then a breath of wind fluted through the open mouths of the bronze lions that guarded the scriptorium roof.

"Is it comet fire?" the Roman legate asked suddenly in low tones, when there was a lull and the soft sky lay quiet and starlit overhead.

Telemakos hesitated. The question had not been addressed to him directly, but Julian had spoken in Latin, so possibly no one else understood him.

But the najashi had once been trained as a translator. "You may answer, Morningstar," said Abreha, speaking flawless Latin himself. "At least, you may address him without seeking my permission. Perhaps there is no answer."

"Is it comet fire?" the legate repeated.

These were San'a's wet months, but nothing like the wintry Long Rains now lashing the Aksumite highlands, and Telemakos was sure he had never seen such a clear night so close to his birthday. Certainly he had never seen such a display straight overhead. His neck ached from the constant craning. Straight through *Cassiopeia's obscure stars*, he thought, remembering a random line of Greek poetry.

"Is it comet fire?"

It's like when I was born, Telemakos thought. It'll be my birth month in a few days. Mother says the stars danced when I was born. But that was before the comet.

Suddenly Telemakos knew what he was seeing.

"It's my Perseids," he cried in sheer unguarded delight. "It's the ancient Perseids! Magus, could it be? There was starfall all the week that I was born, fourteen years ago! By chance we had clear skies that year, as Leo went down to meet the sun—no one's seen the Perseids since. I've never seen them. It was Trinity in the last month of our winter; we're only ten days off! Could it be the Perseids?"

"Where are they?" Dawit asked softly.

"Overhead and a little to the north, in Cassiopeia and Perseus."

The Star Master fished in the depths of his robe and re-
trieved what Telemakos knew to be a worn twig of kat leaves,
the mild stimulant that stained his beard pink. Dawit tore free
several leaves with his teeth and began to chew.

"Aye, it could be the Perseids," he agreed.

All around them, the men gasped and sighed in recogni-
tion and agreement and relief.

"By heaven, he may be right."

"I never thought to see them again, the summers have been
so dismal in the north, since the comet came."

"A sign of better days, perhaps?"

The najashi chuckled softly. "'My *Perseids*,' indeed!" he
echoed Telemakos, fondly mocking. "When did you become
lord of the stars?"

Later, only an hour or two before sunrise, Dawit went with
Telemakos back to the Globe Room and waited for him to put
away the instruments and lay out the wax tablets for transcrip-
tion to hardier palm stalks the next morning. "Two more weeks
and you will be free of your restrictions," Dawit commented. "I
doubt not you are counting down the hours, eh, Lij Bitwoded
Telemakos Eosphorus? What a great mouthful! Beloved young
prince—there is no one else in all Aksum and Himyar with
such a formidable title. I suppose you and I were never formally
introduced, for I had not heard that spoken aloud before."

"I don't think I have, either," Telemakos admitted. He
stacked the tablets slowly, borne down by the weight of his
name. "Not strung end to end like that, anyway. I have

not been 'beloved' very long, only since my accident."

It was his service in Afar that had earned him the bestowed title "Bitwoded," not his mistake in handling the Aksumite emperor's pet lion, but of course he could not say so.

"Well, you have worked hard for your advancement this night," Dawit continued jovially. "Though in truth, the najashi granted it you before you had done anything."

Telemakos looked up. Dawit was nothing but a shadow in the darkness.

"What advancement?"

"You are to act as that Roman's cupbearer at the Assembly feast, are you not?"

"Surely that's only because I speak Latin."

"The najashi dressed you in his own clothes and told a lie on your behalf to spare you a well-deserved humiliation, and then he forced all his guests to *bow to you*. What do you make of *that*, Beloved Young Prince?"

Dawit's robe rustled as he fished for his tired kat leaves. "Abreha has not appointed a cupbearer himself since Asad died. His eldest son." Telemakos heard the Star Master tear off a leaf and begin to chew. Dawit spoke indistinctly around the great wad that was already in his mouth. "You can't pour your own drink from a waterskin. You had better practice."

Telemakos did not mind waiting on people. His grandfather Kidane had long ago taught him to use humility as an indication of good breeding. Telemakos had attended Kidane's special guests as far back as he could remember, and before his accident he had even been called on to serve in the New palace in Aksum; once, to his delight, he had gone as a page on a royal elephant hunt, though it had not been long after his imprisonment in Afar, and they had not let him join in the stalking because he had been so thin.

The feast of Abreha's Great Assembly was held outdoors in one of the stepped gardens. There were canopies over all the braziers and carpets, in case of rain, for it was the time of the summer monsoon. But it was another fine night. San'a's terraces and rocky ledges were at the height of their greenery, with rose of Sharon blooming everywhere and the perfume of jasmine nearly overwhelming. The garden was lit by hundreds of round glass lamps set in crevices up and down the stone sills. Other lights were set on standards in and out among the canopies, and the men of the Great Assembly sat on the carpeted flagstones beneath.

All those burning lamps were fueled by the oil of Gedar's olive groves. When Telemakos came into the garden, he had to close his eyes for one blinding second in a private, hateful sneer. He despised the wasteful light, despised Himyar's prosperity in the wake of plague and war that left Aksum's cities shabby and depleted. And he hated Gedar with a black and bitter hatred: Gedar who had profited by it, Gedar who three years past had taken charity from the house of Nebir while

Telemakos, enslaved in Afar, silently endured having his fingernails pried off to soothe the suspicions of Anako the corrupt governor of Deire.

Arrest Gedar. Telemakos had not heard anything from Aksum for over a month. He could not risk sending this message again. He was torn with guilt for not having tackled a new message about the Hanish Islands.

The men of the Great Assembly sat on the carpeted flagstones beneath the lovely, indifferent lights. Julian, the Roman legate Telemakos had been set to wait upon, was friendly and garrulous. He spoke not a word of South Arabian, but he wanted to know the names of all the men he sat with, and where they came from and the pedigrees of their saluki hounds, how one managed to scratch a living in the desert, and how one might make bitter water drinkable by adding camel's milk to it. He could understand his companions' Greek easily enough, but when he spoke himself it was incomprehensible, so he stuck doggedly to asking his questions in Latin and letting Telemakos translate everything he said.

"I shouldn't be learning half as much without you at my side," the legate confessed to Telemakos as the evening wore on. "What did the Federator Abreha tell us your full name is— Morningstar? Bright Shiner? He honors you near as much as he did Asad, his own son, but you put me in mind of Lleu, Artos's heir, more than you do Asad. Asad was biddable. Lleu had a backbone of steel beneath his winning charm."

"Lleu!" Telemakos exclaimed in surprise, astonished to hear

a foreign stranger speak aloud the name of the dead British prince who haunted his dreams. "How do you know of Lleu?"

"The prince was about your age when I was in Britain. I remember him helping the villagers with the harvest, until they sent him home because he had such trouble breathing. He came back a quarter of an hour later with a cloth tied over his nose to keep out the dust.

"I never met anyone who did not love him," Julian finished warmly. "They called him Leo, the young lion, in Latin. But in their own language he was Lleu, the Bright One, the light-bringer. You see, you even share his name, Beloved Young Prince Lucifer."

Telemakos laughed uneasily. He did not like being held up to his dead uncle for comparison. "They don't call me Lucifer. No one speaks Latin here, as you've heard! It's Athtar, their ancient sky god. Or Eosphorus, in Greek. It's not my real name, only a nickname, because of my light hair. My name is Telema-kos, or young prince, Lij Telemakos, if we must speak formally. Truly, Telemakos is enough."

"And Greek as well, to match Eosphorus! But your Latin is very good."

"The emperor of Aksum was allowed to approve or appoint my tutors," Telemakos said. "He didn't always bother, but it made my mother choose carefully before she employed anyone. My British relatives think I sound like a Byzantine."

"You do," Julian agreed. "There is some Aksumite in your accent, as well, though; you don't sound very British, grandson to Artos and like your uncle though you may be. Well, well. To think that Artos the Dragon has a grandson. Does Constantine the high king of Britain know that Artos has a grandson?"

"Oh, of a surety. He's known me since I was a child. Constantine was ambassador and viceroy in Aksum when my father and my aunt came to stay there."

When Telemakos was six, and his aunt Goewin had first arrived in Aksum, she had threatened to take Telemakos to Britain and set him up as king-in-waiting to rival Constantine. His most vivid memory of Constantine was of a strong hand dragging him mercilessly by the hair through the corridors of the New palace, and then the viceroy's cold voice informing Goewin that he had the right to cut off Telemakos's head. There was no doubt Constantine knew who he was.

"Constantine is my cousin," Telemakos added.

"Close?"

"Once removed." Closer than Queen Muna, he thought; closer than the najashi's children by her would have been. Poor, doomed, biddable Asad wasn't even my blood kin. "Inas of Ma'in says I am related to everybody. I'm also cousin to Gwalchmei of the Orcades, who used to be Constantine's ambassador to the najashi. But I never met Gwalchmei, and a new British emissary has not yet been appointed, so I am all alone here."

"I'm not surprised Abreha drags his heels in appointing a new emissary, after Gwalchmei's carry-on."

"Sir?" Telemakos asked in polite incomprehension. Over

the past three months he had become so schooled in masking his emotions that he did not even lift an eyebrow.

"Gwalchmei was . . . given to sweet deception? Adored by every noblewoman in San'a, shall I say?"

Telemakos laughed, delighted. It was the first clue he had to Gwalchmei's sudden departure from Himyar. "I've not heard that!"

"The king of Himyar is likely refusing the recent choices he's been given for a new ambassador. He'll be wary of any of Gwalchmei's kin, and if necessary he can boast of you as a British representative."

"I am far more Aksumite than British. I don't know anything about Britain other than the names of its rivers." Telemakos paused, and asked politely, "How long were you there? What was the best thing about it, and the worst?"

"Oh—" the legate laughed. "The worst thing about it was the weather, of course. It is supposed to rain all the time, you know, but there was severe drought the year I arrived. And several times since my return to Constantinople, their crops have failed through cold. Constantine sent to us for grain more than once, before Britain's own plague quarantine shut down our trade with them, and just as well, for by then we had none to spare and were importing extra from our najashi here in South Arabia, sitting pretty atop his restored dam in the warmth of the equator. We have suffered, too, since the comet came, even in Byzantium. These past ten years have been cold and dark throughout the northern reaches of the world. Did you hear about the snow in Rome, three years in a row, and frost in summer? It was worse in Britain. But I liked Britain well enough while I was there—skies so vast and near, avenues of ancient stone, and summer evenings of endless light."

Julian looked aslant at Telemakos and held up his cup for more wine.

"Shall you travel there, someday?"

"I don't know. Perhaps." The charm bracelet jangled as Telemakos hefted the wine jar aloft. His daily use of a spear in the najashi's training yards had greatly improved the balance that so eluded him since he had lost his arm. But in preparation for this evening he had filled a thousand goblets, he was sure, with the Star Master acting as his long-suffering gull and pretending he did not mind his robes awash with spilled water. Telemakos was steady now, and though he could not fill the wine jar himself, nor a water bottle for that matter, he could pour from either into a cup. He thought, as he poured now, how strange that he should have come to a point where it was an honor and a triumph to be able to pour out a cup of wine.

I am good at waiting on people, Telemakos thought. It was in waiting on that hyena Anako that I trapped him.

He shivered. Anako again. Oh, if only I could stop *thinking*.

He set the wine jar carefully on the low flagged sill among the scented herbs that grew there, and reached down for the water to mix in Julian's cup. One of the other pages, unthinkingly helpful, had topped up the water jug so that it was now brimful. It was too heavy for Telemakos to pour one-handed. He considered briefly, then knelt and braced the water jar against his thigh. He tipped it slightly to spill away the excess into the herbs, and warm water splashed over his sandaled feet.

Vivid memory clubbed him from out of nowhere, stunning him as brutally as when it had been real. He was at the salt mines; he had accidentally dropped and split open a waterskin, and his sore feet were soothed with an unexpected wash of warm water even as it evaporated in the dry desert air. The *waste*—Telemakos crouched, cowering, with his head tucked into his knees, expecting to be beaten to the ground in punishment.

"*What is it?*"

That was what Anako the Lazarus had said, seeing Telemakos. Not *Who is that?* but *What is it?*—as though Telemakos were such a freak he could not be considered human.

"What is it?"

The voice was real, and a real hand took hold of Telemakos's fingers. He sobbed aloud, as he had never done in Afar, dreading to have to endure the knife beneath his nails again. He choked breathlessly, "Do not, *do not*—"

"Are you ill, child?" the Roman legate asked kindly.

After a long moment, when the piercing blade did not come and no one kicked him, Telemakos looked up. The legate, and the ambassador from the Persian emperor Khosro, and two sheiks of Gharun, stared at Telemakos curiously. Julian had put down his cup. The water jar, thank fortune, had righted itself when Telemakos had witlessly let go of it.

"Are you ill?" Julian repeated.

Telemakos fumed inwardly, furious that he was not able to master himself better. "Your pardon, sir," he gasped aloud. He steadied his voice and managed to speak levelly. "I thought I was going to spill the water. I am inexpert! Please forgive me. I should know to take better care."

He lifted the jug again.

"Your cup, sir?"

Late, late that night, transformed from honored cupbearer to disgraced prisoner once again, beneath the gaze of two vigilant guards, Telemakos made the lengthy climb back to his solitary existence at the height of Ghumdan's towers.

Am I not biddable? he wondered. Have I winning charm and a backbone of steel? Am I really more like Lleu than Asad? Am I at all like either one of them, adored by their kingly fathers? What humiliation, what deprivation, what *cruelty* disguised as discipline, did either one of them ever endure? Blessed and fortunate, what harshness was ever visited on them, those beloved young princes?

Beloved young prince. Telemakos smiled ruefully to himself in the dark as he continued up the endless stairs. That was his own title.

I should expect no mercy, Telemakos supposed, from a man who was imprisoned all his boyhood only because he was the emperor's nephew; a man who saw his elder brother crippled in trying to escape the chains that were forced on him. In one more week, Telemakos told himself, only one more week, my own imprisonment will be over. I will have Athena back. She can help me with my cup. She can hold my pen and paper steady. She likes to comb my hair. And as long as she is at my side, the hideous dreams stay away.

V

THE LION'S BONES

THERE WAS NO ceremony to observe. The morning came when Telemakos stepped outside the scriptorium and found the corridor empty. The guards were gone, and Tharan was not waiting for him. Telemakos was free. He knew he was expected at the spearmen's practice, but he ran straight to the nursery.

Muna and Rasha were setting out a porridge of beans and sesame oil for the children, who were mostly still asleep. Athena, too, was sleeping. She was held in place on her mattress by a pale blue scarf bound around her upper body, but she had managed to twist herself onto her front and slept like a dog, with her knees curled under her stomach and her bottom in the air. One arm had worked free of the swaddling, and she had got her fingers tangled in her hair.

Telemakos laid his cheek against her warm body and closed his eyes, taking in a deep breath of sandalwood and worn cotton and yesterday's yogurt. With trembling fingers he smoothed

Athena's hair. It seemed longer, and less metallic, than he remembered. In three months Athena's childish face had thinned, her legs and arms grown longer. She looked older.

"You have grown, owlet," Telemakos said softly.

"So have you," Muna told him, coming up behind him suddenly.

It was true. The hanging stars in the Great Globe Room brushed the top of his head now, and the smooth skin stretched across the stump of his shoulder itched constantly, in the same way the skin itched beneath the tight silver bracelet. He could get at his shoulder, but not at the bracelet. He had been reduced to worrying it against the door frame, like a bushpig scratching its back on a tree. But Athena would be able to reach it now.

Close by his sister for the first time in weeks, Telemakos could scarcely believe her radiance. Her smooth skin and wild hair were both exactly the color of old honey. Her lashes were as pale as his own, nearly white against her brown skin, and curled like feathers. The features of her pointed face were delicate and narrow, and Telemakos could see his father and mother perfectly balanced there.

"She is very like you," said Muna.

"So my mother said, as well."

Athena began to stir, coughing and yawning and hiccupping and growling as she came awake and got ready to start screaming. With tooth and nail, as quickly as he could, Telemakos attacked the scarf that held her down. He tore the scarf in freeing her.

"Hello, little owlet."

She swarmed into his embrace, shrieking with delight. Lu'lu, who was scarcely three years older than Athena, sat up in the other small bed. She glanced dismissively at Athena as if no performance could surprise her anymore, then got up, took up her dress where it lay folded neatly on the clothesbox, and with sugary docility held it up to Rasha to help her put it on. Lu'lu did not look at Telemakos. He thought she must have forgotten who he was, until he remembered that Abreha's Royal Scions had all vowed not to get him in trouble by trying to talk to him. Lu'lu was carefully keeping to her vow.

"Let me go for just a moment, Tena—"

Athena held on to his hair with her fists and rubbed her nose against his, and tried to explain the whole of the last three months in one great burst of babbling speech. "Athena's boy, you see my lion, see my baby lion, big lion, see my birds," she said. "Lu'lu can eat the rice not Athena, Tena rice big mess. Muna does not like to carry me. Shadi's big bird gone now, Shadi crying. Open najashi's box, Athena see boy's animals. You see my big lion?"

"Ah, little Athena—" He was astounded at how articulate she had become. It made him want to weep, all he had missed.

"See my window broken, boy see," Athena said, with undue pride. She pulled at his shamma shawl. "You come see it—"

"All right, which way is it?"

"You carry me." She stood on his legs and put her arms around his neck.

"I can't carry you, you're a big girl!" He could no longer lift her with one arm, or not for long, anyway. "Aren't you a walking girl?" She seemed so grown up.

"She doesn't walk," Muna said quietly.

"You carry me, boy. Carry Tena's belt." Athena scurried on hands and feet, agile and lionlike, to one of the cedarwood chests. She banged on it with her fists. "Fetch Athena's belt, Rasha," she commanded imperiously.

Muna's haughty attendant obeyed this command in silence. She opened the chest and took out the child's harness that Medraut had made for Telemakos so that he could carry Athena on his hip without having to get help from anyone. Rasha crossed the room and gave the saddle to Telemakos. No one had oiled it, or even touched it, in all the months of Telemakos's confinement. Telemakos kneaded the stiff leather, stretching out the seams and pockets. When he checked between the folds of the pouch within the seat, the one Athena could not get at herself, his fingers touched paper and silver. There were half a dozen vials and sachets of opium still hidden there.

I must get rid of this, Telemakos thought. She will soon be clever enough to pull things out of here.

"*It is he!*" Malika cried. The queen of Sheba was standing in the door to the nursery, her gown back-to-front. She must

have put it on herself, a wonder indeed, in her hurry to be first
with the news.

She called delightedly over her shoulder to the other Scions, "It is, it is the Aksumite prince, the Morningstar is back
among us!" Then she threw herself down on the carpet at his
side and rattled her fingers through the silver charms he wore.

"Peace to you, Morningstar, peace and greetings and hurrah!
I heard your little bells and I knew you were in here—it sounded
so much closer than when you pass in the corridor. Pretty, aren't
these? Look, little Tena, you can make these bells ring."

Malika held him still with one friendly hand on his shoulder.
She rubbed noses with him as she rattled the silver charms.

"This is *so lovely*! You lucky thing. The najashi has never
given me such a pretty bauble."

Inas and Shadi came in now, laughing and exclaiming in
outrage. "Liar! What about your onyx box of facepaints—"

"—Your cameos, your carnelian earrings? Good morning
and good fortune to you, Morningstar!"

Telemakos knelt, hugging Athena against him, rather
stunned, as the nursery filled with Abreha's fourteen foster
children, all clamoring around him in high-spirited welcome.
He almost thought they must be teasing him.

"Look at your brother's bracelet, Athena bird girl, it's like
yours! You can match now. Rasha, where's the baby's silver
bracelet? Let her wear it so they can both have one."

"Have you heard all your sister's exploits, how she poured a
jar of indigo dye all over the cushions by the window—"

"And of the time she set free the whole great cage of Indian parrots—"

"And an owl was eating them, it had taken three that were perching in the walled almond garden, and Shadi caught it with his new bird?"

The thin, dark boy king gave a proud and quiet smile. "My sparrowhawk, she means. And on another day, Athena pulled two of the strings out of Muna's lyre and cut her hands on them. And on another day, she tipped two lamp stands over the terrace wall, all ablaze—"

"My Athena!" Telemakos exclaimed, and kissed her springing bronze hair. "How can so small a girl commit such enormous knavery?"

"Trees and flowers on fire," she said proudly. "Birds flying away." She let Rasha fasten her silver seabird bracelet about her wrist and gave it a shake. "Flying birds!" She gripped Telemakos by the hair with one hand on either side of his head and gazed into his face anxiously. "Stay with Athena."

"Yes, stay with us awhile," said Inas. "Or have you some prince's duty you must attend to straight away?"

"Javelin practice."

"We'll come with you," said Malika. "We can watch. It will stop Athena making a fuss if we all go down together."

Telemakos saw, with envy, that they were now wiser in the ways of Athena than he was, and decided not to argue. And anyway, he wanted to take her with him. He did not want to let her go.

Telemakos pulled the leather straps of her harness over his head and let Athena climb in it herself. The bands were tighter than they had been, and Athena waited impatiently while, with some difficulty, he adjusted the buckles. She kicked at his ribs and thumped his ruined shoulder with her fist.

"Birds, lion, dogs, goats!" Athena demanded. The Scions all laughed at her.

"Dictating the itinerary again, bird girl?" Inas teased. "We will visit all your friends."

"I want to see the lion and the dogs, too," Telemakos told his sister. He was aching to see them.

The najashi himself turned up at the close of that morning's javelin practice. He stood with folded arms, splendid in his council robes, frowning blackly beneath the rope of gold that bound his headcloth. He looked like God come along to observe the day's human activities in Eden. He left before the session was finished, without speaking to Telemakos, but he stopped among the Scions for some time, as he always did, and Telemakos could hear his unexpectedly merry laughter break free as they spoke to him.

Tharan said to Telemakos afterward, "You may forgo the riding ring today. The najashi bids you spend an hour or so in the kennels and see if the lion still remembers you. You may go hawking with the princes Shadi and Jibril, later, if you wish."

It was turning into a holiday after all.

The Scions stuck to him like honey. They could not have made a plainer statement of their loyalty if they had made formal pledges on their knees in the parade ground before the city walls. Shadi and tall Jibril fell into step on either side of him like lieutenants, and at their shoulders came the desert cousins Ibrahim and Nabil and Numair, demon riders all. Numair walked so lightly on his toes he seemed to have springs in his heels. He had been grinning quietly to himself since Abreha's visit.

"What're you so pleased with?" Telemakos asked.

"We get to see you master the lion. Fabulous show! I've missed it."

Behind them came the girls, Inas and proud Malika; then Nadia and Nashita, arm in arm and whispering like conspirators as always, with Lu'lu, the spoiled littlest of them, clinging to Nashita's dress. The four younger boys followed them as rearguard: quarrelsome Haytham and his younger brother Habib; Inas's younger brother Amir, who was by inheritance king of Ma'in; and Wajih, good-natured and nearly spherical in shape, heir to the great citadel port at Aden and all its lands and riches. Telemakos always thought of Wajih as being three times his age; it was so easy to picture him as the oversized, benevolent king he would be in twenty years, bearded and turbaned and sceptered, being fed like Gebre Meskal's old aunt Candake by a host of attendants.

Twenty years. Will they all visit each other, and send each other presents, trade indigo and coffee and grain and frankincense, go to war together, send representatives to San'a every year for the Great Assembly? Will they remember me?

Telemakos could not imagine what he would be in twenty years.

The lion was at play in the hounds' racetrack. Menelik seemed twice as big as he had been a season ago; he was bigger than Telemakos now, though still not anywhere near the impressive weight of his sire, Solomon, who ruled the lion pit in the New palace in Aksum. His mane had begun to grow. There was no length to it yet, but it shimmered like a black film creeping around his golden head and down the fur at the back of his strong neck. He was tossing about a strange rattle made of bones all knotted together with rope; the thing looked like an enormous white spider and made a riotous hollow rattling noise as the young lion worried and shook it. Telemakos stood at the gate to the arena, watching Menelik toss the rattling bones into the air and catch them in his mouth.

Athena called out, "Lion lion lion lion!" and chirruped deep and loud. It was exactly the sound Menelik himself made in greeting. The lion came bounding over to the gate, the bone rattle in his mouth. He dropped the bones and rubbed his head adoringly against the bolted wood, chirping like an oversized kitten. Telemakos reached over the gate, without thinking, to scratch the lion between the ears, and Menelik began to purr.

"Oh, still so easily won!" Telemakos laughed, delighted.

"You throw it, you throw my lion's toy," Athena told him.

"Let's have it. Let's see how well they've trained you without me. Give me the bones! Give!"

Menelik picked up the rattle in his teeth and held it up to Telemakos.

"Good, good—let go! Give!"

Telemakos took hold of one of the long, scarred bones. They were heavy; the rackety bundle weighed nearly as much as Athena.

"Bring it back!"

With a thunder of bone and a sweet shower of silver chimes, Telemakos hurled the rattle with all the strength he would have put behind a javelin cast. The bone spider sailed, clattering across the track. Menelik raced after it, subdued it as it crashed into the far wall, then picked up the thing daintily by a single bone and came loping back to Telemakos in deadly silence.

"He's a good lion," Athena said approvingly.

Telemakos stared. The heavy young king Wajih whistled through his teeth.

"I shouldn't want to turn my back on *him*!"

"Indeed not," Telemakos agreed, breathless with astonishment. "That's how I lost my arm, to his father. Give, Menelik, give me the bones."

Telemakos threw them again, and again the white sticks stormed through the air, and again Menelik brought them back without a sound.

Telemakos watched the lion run, his own heart racing with discovery.

He moves with it, Telemakos thought. *He moves with it!* Look at him! I can't pick that thing up without a riot, but when the lion wants to muffle it, there's not a sound. Yes, I see, he doesn't let it fall still, he lets the bones shake from side to side, but as long as he keeps moving, they don't knock against each other.

"Again again again!" Athena crowed.

Telemakos shook his bracelet tentatively. He reached toward the lion, thinking only of silencing the bells at his elbow.

Yes, I *can* do it. Not well, not yet. But if I practice, if I practice!

Telemakos collared the lion affectionately by the scruff of its neck. Menelik pushed up his heavy head for kisses, as he had done since he was a starving kit fed on milk from a goatskin.

"Oh, you *baby*!" Telemakos exclaimed. He leaned over the gate and gave the required kiss. The young lion smelled warm and familiar, of straw and sun and honey. "Ah, thank you for this instruction," Telemakos whispered in the lion's ear.

"What is a mother?" Athena asked, sitting wide awake in the darkness of the Great Globe Room long after the rest of the palace was asleep.

"Why, a mother . . ."

Telemakos found himself at a loss. Athena did not remember her own mother. He did not want her to think Muna was her mother.

"A mother makes children," Telemakos said. "A mother and father together make a child."

It made no sense. None of the Scions had a mother or father; they were all dead of plague.

"Sometimes after the child is made, the mother and father are not able to take care of it. So they have to get help from someone else. Queen Muna takes care of children who have no mother. You have got a mother, but she lives too far away to take care of you, so Muna helps. You have got a father, too."

"Are you my father?"

Telemakos laughed. "I am your brother."

"What is a brother?"

"Oh, save me, Tena, it is time to sleep!"

She bounced in the cushions and repeated patiently, "What is a brother?"

"Your brother has the same mother and father as you. They look after you together. Or you and your brother look after each other. Inas has got a little brother, Amir. You know Amir."

"Is Menelik my brother?"

"Of course he is not, you silly thing. Menelik is a *lion!*"

They both laughed.

"You are full of difficult questions tonight, little Tena," Telemakos said.

"Menelik is like my brother," she said.

"I know," Telemakos whispered, thinking of the silent bones. "He is like my brother, too."

Athena slept pressed tight against his side that night, and every night after that. A semblance of peace fell on the Ghumdan palaces.

VI

ALLIANCES

NOW TELEMAKOS HAD a secret that he took delight in. He was learning to move without making any noise. He practiced when he was alone or when he was working with the lion; nobody ever noticed whether his charm bracelet was ringing, if the lion was there to hold everyone's attention. He could not throw a spear without rattling the charms, but before long he could walk and run in silence. He could move as quietly as Menelik if he wanted to. And this challenge, more than anything else, finally restored his sense of balance.

He could not get enough of being outside. He knew he was watched like a goat; he was always minded at a distance by a herdsman, or two or three. He did not pass the city gates without an escort of the najashi's soldiers. They kept their distance, and if any of the Scions were with him, Telemakos did not see his more formal escort at all, but Telemakos knew he was watched carefully, all the time. People knew who he was. In San'a's suq markets he once let Athena choose a set of ivory hairpins for their mother, and experimentally tried to send them off with a note dictated through an itinerant letter writer. The old man would not take his message.

"The Ghumdan palace children should use the Ghumdan palace servants," the scribe grumbled. "You can have no need of a street writer."

"I bought this gift in the street," Telemakos said. "Why can't I also send it in the street?"

"No paid scribe will risk his hands and livelihood in forwarding unapproved messages for foreign princes."

"Your pardon, sir," Telemakos apologized. "I would not compromise anyone's livelihood."

"You may send the gift without a message," said the writer.

Telemakos did not care that he was watched. He could go where he liked. The semblance of freedom was even better than his other recent joy: that of running or riding in the chase with the royal saluki hounds, gripping one spear for balance and with two more strapped to his back should he spend the first, and the najashi allowing him to lead the hunt with Menelik at his side.

Street children and beggars still stared and cringed at his white hair and strange eyes, but the Scions rallied to his defense.

"Your majesty of Qataban!" the almond pickers called out in greeting to Shadi as they passed through the groves beyond the city gates when Telemakos went hawking with the more senior of Abreha's collection of royal orphans. "What are you doing in the company of that half-breed Aksumite? Don't you know those blue eyes can curse you?"

Another boy in the same tree added, "Aye, and are the najashi's Royal Scions now set to playing nursemaid, that the Aksumite comes hunting with a baby tied to his back like a woman?"

Shadi, who was slight of build and cautious of temper, raised the sparrowhawk on his wrist a fraction and stood gazing up at the boys in the tree.

"I had not judged you such fools, Hujir and Yazid," he said at last. There was rustling among the leaves as the young workers within earshot stopped to listen. One dropped out of the branches so he could better see the confrontation.

"The najashi himself is Aksumite, and his Socotran queen is blue eyed," Shadi said amiably, "so have a care with your insults. As to the Morningstar, he is our guide and a captain among us, and since he has no falcon to fly, he may carry his sister with him if he likes."

Shadi turned to Telemakos.

"Why don't you make a pledge not to curse anyone with those evil eyes of yours? Swear by your remaining hand."

"By this hand," Telemakos swore solemnly. He had not realized Shadi could be such a performer. He bit his lip and covered his evil eyes, so the local boys would not have to look at them while he swore.

"You may pass the word along the treetops," Shadi said.

"The Morningstar is one of us. Our guide and captain." He flung a silver coin into the basket of almond fruits that stood beneath the tree, and added, as a parting shot, "The Morningstar does not have a hawk, but he does not need one. He has his sister, and she is better than a hawk."

Athena was, indeed, the bloodiest hunter among them.

"Bird in the grass," she would whisper, one finger up by her cheek, pointing carefully to a red-legged partridge shuffling through the tall brush of the savannah. "Fat fat fat! You get that one, Boy." She would call to it alluringly in perfect imitation of its own chuckling cluck, and then she would hand to Telemakos a stone for his sling. Sometimes he did not even notice her retrieving them from the pockets of her saddle; she was always ready with them when he needed them. She was as obsessed with accuracy as her marksman father, and judged Telemakos's shots critically.

"Too low. That hen is scared now; Shadi can get it with his big bird."

Once she was so angry with Telemakos for missing that she began to pound him in the face, brutally, with both small fists. Short of hitting back, he could do nothing to stop her, as they were bound together. The other boys had to come to his aid and prise her off him. They got the buckles of the harness undone and lifted Athena away, kicking and screaming, and set her on the ground. Telemakos found himself shaking like an empty wasp's nest in the wind. His fingers scarcely obeyed him as he wound up his sling and fumbled to hook it back into his

belt. It occurred to him for the first time that, for his own protection, Athena's wild temper might need to be trained. A few
drops of water spilled over his feet could transport him back to
Afar as a quivering prisoner; being beaten over the head could
do the same or worse.

"Shadi will carry you home," Telemakos told Athena as
coolly as he could, and tucked his disheveled hair back behind
his ears. "Or you can scamper back yourself. I won't carry such
a monster."

She wailed in outrage, "Boy! Athena's boy carry me! No,
not Shadi—" She pulled herself up to stand, hugging Telemakos around the legs. But he was still trembling, and it took all
his will not to push her away.

"Listen, Athena, these are your choices," he said levelly.
"Shadi carries you, or nobody carries you. What are you going
to choose?"

"I choose *you*, Boy," she said stubbornly.

"*Telemakos*," he snapped in deep and uncontrolled frustration. "Why do you never call me by my name? I am *Telemakos*."

Shadi came suddenly to Athena's defense. "Nobody calls
you Telemakos," he pointed out. "Why should she? The Star
Master calls you 'boy,' too."

Telemakos prised himself free of his little sister's hands. "I'll
carry you tomorrow. Let go. You may not hit me. You choose
Shadi, or nobody."

"*You*."

"Shadi or nobody."

"*Shadi,*" she muttered ominously.

"Good choice."

Telemakos held Athena by the back of an arm to keep her from clutching at him again, and made her sit.

"You wait here while I take Shadi's hawk. Behave yourself, or this bird may hurt me, for I don't know how to tell it what to do." Telemakos was inspired with a threat that she would take seriously. "If you hit Shadi or pull his hair, I will tell the najashi not to let you play with his salukis for a week. No dogs if you hurt Shadi, do you understand? Mother of God! It's bad enough my father and Tharan clouting me over the head for my poor aim, without my baby sister doing it as well."

"Which way back?" Jibril asked him.

Telemakos did not know what he had done to deserve the Scions calling him their captain, but it was true that he was their guide. As trackers they were witless. Beyond the cultivated orchards and olive groves, wild grasslands ran north and east and west to the barren al-Surat Mountains, and not one of Abreha's Scions ever came here unescorted. Indeed, some of them never went out of the palace unescorted. Telemakos, who had roamed the streets of Aksum freely from the moment he had been big enough to climb over his grandfather's garden wall, sometimes found it hard not to laugh at Jibril's complete lack of any sense of direction. Jibril had once managed to get himself locked outside the city gates after curfew.

"We follow this irrigation ditch back to where the three stone culverts meet, and the city road is just beyond."

"You seem to hold all the world in your head."

"It is hammered into me daily."

Shadi's sparrowhawk was, thankfully, more cooperative than Athena, who sniffled and sulked as Shadi fixed her to his side in Telemakos's harness. Jibril stroked the hawk's downy barred belly with a fingertip to help Telemakos settle it on his wrist. Telemakos walked carefully as they started back toward the road, as though he were carrying a basket on his head. Jibril stayed close by him.

"I can make you a map of the roads around the city," Telemakos offered. "And the hunting grounds."

"Thank you," Jibril said without any enthusiasm, as though that was not really what he wanted. Telemakos glanced sideways at him. Jibril did not look so much lost as obdurate.

"Well then, what? I would like to help."

"You have the najashi's favor," Jibril said, his voice low.

"I don't have the najashi's favor," Telemakos protested, speaking low as well, mindful of the unfamiliar hawk perched on his forearm. "I have his attention. Most of the time I am branded as a sneak and an eavesdropper. You've seen! I am only ever allowed to tie up these cursed charms when I go hunting, and I may not hunt alone. The najashi binds them himself, in his study, before I leave the palace, and the sentries at the gate have orders to unwrap the bells before I am allowed back in. I have lost the najashi's trust."

Jibril laughed. "Oh, of a surety, you have lost his trust. And so he names you beloved cupbearer, and trains you to hunt and to ride and to fight, and gives you opium whenever you need it, and indulges you when you bring your baby sister to his feasts or his councils or wherever you like, and follows your advice when you tell him which of his principalities to marry together!"

"Follows my advice!" Telemakos echoed, taken aback. "Is that true? Shadi, king of Qataban!" he called out, glancing behind him. "Has the najashi changed his mind about who is to marry Malika?"

"So she boasts," said Shadi gruffly, hurrying to catch up with them. He had hold of Athena's feet, one in each hand, to stop her kicking him. "Ah-la-la," he hummed tunelessly at her ear. Telemakos began to understand how the Scions' puzzling loyalty had taken root.

"I heard it, too," Jibril said. "When last the najashi came hawking with us himself, I heard his lieutenant talking about it. And I wondered . . ."

Jibril hesitated yet again.

". . . I wondered if you might find out what he plans for my future, now that I have come of age and have pledged him my service. I dread the day I must return to my father's brother in Kinda, who neglects the tithe he owes to the najashi, and sends out raids against my mother's tribe. How can I unite them for the Federation, I who have no skill with words or weapons?"

They walked the windy grasslands in silence, except for

Athena's occasional self-pitying sniffs. Telemakos kept his attention on the sparrowhawk, thinking.

"You want me to speak to Abreha on your behalf."

"You helped Malika and Shadi."

"So you did," Shadi agreed.

Telemakos turned the names of kingdoms over in his head, as though he were memorizing the names of rivers or stars: Sheba and Qataban, Sheba and Qataban. He could see their outlines spread on the world as they spread on a map, the green terraced hillsides rich with frankincense and grain, the torrid ports beyond the narrow straits that guarded the Red Sea.

I could make a collection, Telemakos thought, of tribute owed me by Himyar's rising generation. Which is Jibril's kingdom—Kinda? How will Abreha go on playing God with me when I am able to twist debts of loyalty out of Sheba, Qataban, and Kinda? That's a quarter of his kingdom.

"Perhaps the najashi might arm you, now that you've reached manhood," Telemakos said slowly. "You could train with the young soldiers, as I do. Then you will have some standing when you return to your tribe."

"I would be indebted to you."

"I won't forget," Telemakos said, smiling. "I'll tell him."

It was well into Himyar's dry winter months then, the traveling season, and still Telemakos had no letters from his father or his aunt. But his mother wrote to him at last:

A sad thing has happened to our neighbors. Gedar is discovered to have had a large store of salt illegally acquired during the quarantine, and also stands accused of other petty thefts and piracies, so he has been arrested and fined and put to labor. The emperor has been merciful to his family, though. He has taken the children in as pages, and allowed their mother to go away to live with her sister. The villa opposite our house stands empty now. Perhaps Abreha has already told you this sad news, for I know that Gedar used to supply all the najashi's lamp oil.

Your aunt Goewin sends you greetings, and also your father.

VII

A GAME OF JACOB'S DREAM

"THE BRITISH AMBASSADOR is back," said Shadi. "I saw the najashi showing him the falcons, when Jibril and I were down yesterday."

"It wasn't the British ambassador." Quarrelsome Haytham, who was by birth king of Awsan, spoke quickly. "It was a white man, but it wasn't Gwalchmei. It was an older man, and taller, and Gwalchmei's hair was red, not moonlight fair."

"He looked like Gwalchmei," said Shadi. "Gwalchmei with silver hair. Gwalchmei's beard was silver-fair, remember? Maybe his hair's gone white, too. He would be older now."

"He couldn't be *taller*, could he?" Haytham derided.

"Who else has such hair?"

Telemakos caught his breath. He was idly stringing wooden beads with Athena, holding up a leather lace for her to thread them on, but he was listening intently as always to everything the fourteen Scions said. Head bent, watching through his lashes, he could see all of Abreha's foster children turn to gaze at him as if in obvious answer to Shadi's idiotic question.

"It's Ras Meder, Medraut son of Artos, Medraut of Britain," said Jibril.

Telemakos carefully let out the held breath, too steeled to disappointment to allow himself to believe this news, yet half expecting it. For nearly a year he had been hiding secrets in everything he wrote, and he had immediately seen the double meaning in the cryptic close of his mother's letter: *Your aunt sends greetings, and also your father.*

Athena held the leather lace upside down so that all the beads slid off.

"Who is it?" she asked. "Who is coming? Who is Ras Meder?"

Telemakos gazed at her in guilty sorrow. "Ras Meder is our father," he said. "Yours and mine." He should have taught her her father's name by now. She ought to know her father's name, and her mother's.

Malika turned on him with accusation in her voice.

"You didn't tell us your father was on his way here, Morningstar."

"I didn't know," Telemakos answered, and could not stop his heart leaping with excitement and sudden hope. "I've had no more than two letters from him since I arrived in San'a. If he's here, it's not on my account."

"That's so," said Jibril. "He wants to be the new British ambassador."

But three days passed, and still Telemakos never saw Medraut, and would not have known he was there if the Scions had not told him so.

On the third morning he saw that his father was sitting with the najashi on one of the upper terraces during the young spearmen's target practice, watching him. Telemakos's aim went all to hell after that. Tharan, in disgust, put him to shame by setting him to retrieving spent spears.

Telemakos went to see the lion later that afternoon; lions always consoled him. Telemakos was too tall now to ride on Menelik's back as he used to with the lion Solomon, but Athena could. Telemakos held her in place and she clung to the short black tufts of Menelik's new mane. The young lion walked sedately around the dogs' racetrack with Athena sitting astride his shoulders.

"Lie down," she commanded in South Arabian, and Menelik obediently crouched with his belly against the sandy floor and let her climb off. No one, not even Telemakos, could command the lion the way Athena did.

"I want to go hunting," she said.

"You do. You come hawking with Shadi and Jibril."

"I want to go hunting with Menelik."

"You are too little."

"The dogs may go," she pointed out, as though she ought to enjoy any privilege a saluki enjoyed.

Telemakos slung her carrying saddle over his shoulders and knelt down so she could climb into it. She had learned to fasten the buckles herself, much more efficiently than he could. Telemakos climbed to his feet and together they followed the kennelmen around as the dogs were fed. The newest litter were all nursing, and Telemakos lingered over them covetously, making up the names he would give them if they were his own.

"Argos," he told Athena. "That's what Odysseus's dog was called, and I am named after Odysseus's son."

"Shams," Athena said, the name of the ancient South Arabian goddess of the sun. There was no telling where she had heard it. She was becoming such a Himyarite.

"Selene," he said. "That's the old Greek goddess of the moon. You'll have to learn to speak Greek, soon, or everyone at home will think you are terribly ignorant."

"Selene," Athena repeated agreeably, because she liked the sound. "Selene, Selene. Athena's dog Selene!"

"They're not our dogs really, little Tena." They never would be: the salukis were nearly sacred, owned strictly by nobility, so prized and honored they could never be sold, only given as gifts. "You can say Selene so nicely, little Athena," Telemakos said wistfully. "When are you going to learn to say Telemakos?"

But he knew it was a word she never heard unless he spoke it himself.

On their way back up to the children's room, they met Abreha in the tiled walkway that connected the kennels with the main courtyard. The sun was setting beyond the mountains, lighting the tops of San'a's towers, though the city's streets already lay in shadow. Points of colored light were beginning to gleam in the high windows.

"Najashi! Najashi!" Athena waved wildly. "I was riding on the lion!"

Abreha came to meet them.

"I've missed your lion-taming show again, my honey badger," the najashi said amiably, falling into step with Telemakos. "Your brother must send me warning next time he brings you down here, and I will come and watch."

"Is Ras Meder a prisoner?" Telemakos asked abruptly.

The najashi laughed. "Assuredly he is not! Why should he be, O distrustful one?"

"You will not let me see him."

"Your father is an emissary for the emperor. He is the message bearer in a negotiation with my cousin."

Darkness began to swallow the yard. An owl called, and Athena answered it. The najashi's look beneath his heavy brow seemed murderous in the dusk, but his voice was mild. "Last year the emperor Gebre Meskal arrested a servant of mine, and through him discovered what you discovered, that secret shipments of salt were made during the plague years between Aksum and Himyar in defiance of Aksum's quarantine. Gebre Meskal is, as you have assured me, a forgiving despot. He offers to make peace with me, through a compensation. Gebre Meskal will forgive me my coercion if I relinquish my claim on the Hanish Archipelago."

"And will you?"

"On condition he allows me to map Hanish for myself, and allows me custody of certain men imprisoned there who have served me loyally."

That meant Anako the Lazarus, the man who had tortured Telemakos in Afar. Telemakos shuddered. Athena pulled at his hair absently, hoo-hooing softly over his shoulder at the owl that called from the hanging gardens.

"If all this comes to pass," Telemakos said slowly, "the secrets I stole from you will no longer be secret. Will you then destroy the warrant you keep in your sash, and allow me someday to walk free of your kingdom?"

"Free of my stricture, perhaps," said Abreha. "But do you truly despise my kingdom so?"

"Do you really carry my death warrant in your sash at all times?" Telemakos asked.

The lamplighters were coming through the courtyard now, and shadows sprang dancing to life. Abreha reached into his waistband and drew out the document Telemakos had seen him hide there a year ago. The lock of Telemakos's hair that sealed it caught the torchlight for half a second, glinting silver.

"Najashi, najashi, that's the Boy's hair." Athena reached for the shining silver.

"Do not touch," said the najashi sharply, and Athena snatched her hands back into little fists, staring up at him with her clear gray eyes wide. Then she remembered to look away.

"You truly are a tyrant," Telemakos said bitterly.

"I am no tyrant," Abreha answered him, and his voice was

hard as frost. "I pass no law over my land that is not approved by the majority of tribes in my Federation. I am in Solomon's palace as their federator only because they nominated me to this reign. I cannot even appoint my own heir without their approval." The najashi slapped Telemakos lightly across the face with the sealed parchment. "I hold you in jeopardy because you have knowledge that threatens my Federation. You yourself have pointed out you are not sworn to serve me. No man can serve two masters. How can I trust you to visit with your father? What will Medraut of Britain think of me, if I must stop his brave son's mouth with cloth before they may see each other?"

Abreha folded the parchment back into his belt. He walked on, leaving Telemakos to follow.

"Don't cry, Boy," Athena said in the motherly voice she copied from Inas.

Athena was not in the nursery all the next day. No one brought her up to the Globe Room to build towers with the wax tablets, or practice counting on Dawit's intriguing abacus from Cathay. Anger and abandonment began to wrap choking coils about Telemakos's throat. He managed to ask polite permission from the Magus to eat supper with the Scions, and stormed down to the children's room with the silver alarm bells sending crashing echoes up and down the stairwell. Sometimes, when he found himself shaking with pent fury, he made as much noise with them as he could.

Rasha, the queen's haughty handmaid, stood holding the door open for him.

"*Where is Athena?*"

"With the najashi. He has kept her by him all this day."

"And with my father? *With my father*, am I right? Why only the baby, why not me as well? Ras Meder wouldn't even look at her, most of her first year alive! Why hasn't he sent for *me?*" His voice cracked plaintively over the final word, and he coughed to cover it.

Rasha looked past him, into the room, to where Muna was presiding over the children's meal.

"You surely know the najashi has not allowed it," Rasha said sharply, in a crisp, clipped voice. "At any rate you have not been singled out for disapproval, Morningstar, because my lady Muna has been banished from his presence as well. Medraut of Britain is welcome to visit with his daughter, but not with his son; welcome to visit with the najashi, but not with the najashi's queen. Who can fathom the najashi's rulings?"

She ushered Telemakos into the room and closed the door behind them. Muna looked up. Her strange blue-green Socotran eyes were pink rimmed. "Don't mock the boy, Rasha," she said quietly. "He has a right to wonder." She turned her pale gaze on Telemakos. After a pause she said, "When supper is finished, we will go together to see your father. You are to bring your linen maps to show him, those you've been making for the Star Master to read. Rasha, get me a veil ready; I shall go formally dressed."

She led Telemakos downstairs to Abreha's apartment without speaking, lighting their way with an old alabaster lamp shaped like an ibex. Telemakos felt like a conspirator. Muna was demure, not defiant, and Telemakos had never known her to cross her husband in anything. But Telemakos felt that he was doing something faintly illicit, following the white-gold light and the faint glitter of Muna's dress through the labyrinthine marble stairways of Solomon's ancient palace. When Muna glanced back at him, only her eyes were visible above the veil, and he seemed to be following a stranger.

And all the way down the steps he worried at the thought: I must tell Ras Meder about the Hanish Islands. I must tell him about the plot against the emperor's armada. How can I do it? The najashi will never leave us alone together. He said he'd stop my mouth.

In the najashi's reception room Medraut and the Star Master sat cross-legged, facing each other. Medraut had his hands spread before him, holding up a complicated maze of looped thread; Dawit was picking and pulling the pattern into a new design, his sensitive fingers counting lines and spaces while his milky eyes stared straight ahead in concentration. Watching them, deeply absorbed, Athena sat quietly in the najashi's lap. On either side of Medraut an attendant waited, alert, each poised on one knee with his fists closed against his chest.

Muna went in first. Telemakos stood on the threshold behind her, hardly daring to breathe. Dawit heard them there and looked toward them vacantly. "Welcome at last, Morningstar," he said. "The baby kept pulling at her father's hair, because it looks like yours, so we thought she would like a string game.

We are telling the story of Jacob's dream." He lifted the strings from Medraut's hands, pulled his own hands apart, and made the thread go taut and tight into a new pattern of three interlocking stars. "Come in, come in."

Medraut sat back and rested one arm idle across a raised knee. The familiar odd, critical half smile played about the corner of his mouth as he watched Telemakos come forward. Telemakos met his smoke-blue gaze steadily; Medraut and Goewin, alone of all the adults he knew, demanded his respect by forcing him to look them directly in the eye.

White skinned, white haired, Medraut seemed impossibly alien in the najashi's chambers, and Telemakos realized suddenly that his father was dressed as a British native. Medraut's kilt and tunic were of some dark, soft animal skin, and his boots were of the same stuff, supple and shining; over his shoulders hung a swath of fine wool, like a shamma but wrapped differently, woven in a chessboard pattern of blocks of green and blue and brown and gray. The cloak was pinned with a gold brooch in the shape of a snarling dragon. There was a knot of gold in his earlobe, and his pale hair was swept back into a single plait.

He looks like a king, Telemakos thought. If he were wearing a crown, you would mistake him for the high king of Britain. He is more regal than the najashi himself.

Medraut lifted his hand toward Telemakos in mute command. Telemakos suppressed the babyish urge to burst into tears and dive sobbing into his father's arms; he understood that

Medraut wanted Telemakos to acknowledge him with a formal greeting. Telemakos knelt before his father. He laid down the rolled maps that he carried, took the offered hand, and kissed it courteously. At Telemakos's side, again like his conspirator, Muna also knelt. Telemakos held fast to his father's hand.

"Look, Boy, that is the Ras," said Athena helpfully. "The prince."

"Ras Meder," Telemakos agreed.

"That is our mother the prince."

The Star Master spluttered with laughter. His fingers were still webbed in the string stars, waiting for Medraut to take his next turn at them.

Telemakos bit his lip. "You mean *father*, little Tena. He is our father."

Athena wriggled out of the najashi's lap and shuffled across the carpet to sit between Telemakos and the queen. "The Ras has got a snake in his hand."

Medraut, still smiling his faint smile, tolerantly turned over the stiff fingers of his left hand to reveal the tattooed serpent hidden in his palm.

"I know, Tena," Telemakos said. "I have seen it before. My lord—Sir—" The word came out as a ridiculous squeak. Telemakos choked, and swallowed. "Peace to you, Ras Meder, and welcome to San'a."

"Indeed," Medraut said dryly, and raised his chin with the slightest jerk, as if in defiance.

There was a fine chain wrapped twice about his throat.

Telemakos had at first thought it to be a fastening of his cloak. It was of iron, not ornamental; its tails were thrown back over Medraut's shoulders. Telemakos saw now that each of the kneeling attendants held an end of the chain. If they pulled on it, they would choke Medraut.

Still clasping his father's hand, Telemakos turned to Abreha, lips parted in disbelief. Medraut, also, glanced at the najashi. Fixed by the twin bores of their cold, steel stares, Abreha lowered his eyes.

"My Morningstar," the najashi said quietly, "there are things your father must not tell you. You cannot know how deeply it shames me to have to hold him in such durance. But we cannot come to an agreement about what you should and should not know, and the days fly past without you seeing each other. I swear you do not need one more scrap of dangerous knowledge in your head."

Medraut withdrew his hand. Telemakos sat back on his heels before his father, glaring murderously at the najashi. "Do you treat all your ambassadors like this?"

Athena crept closer to Telemakos. She recognized a battle when she saw one, and she wanted to be sure Telemakos's anger was not directed at her. She climbed up to lean against Telemakos, with one hand in his hair and the other twisting the neck of his shirt.

"I will not have your father as my ambassador," Abreha answered evenly.

Out of the corner of his vision Telemakos saw Muna dip

her head aside as she sat back on her heels as well. Her gossamer veil covered her nose and mouth, and the silk shimmered and caught the light as she moved her head. Her eyes glittered pale green above the veil.

She never goes veiled, Telemakos thought. None of the Himyar women do. A Byzantine noblewoman might, I suppose, if she were being terribly formal. Why has Muna veiled herself for my father?

The najashi spoke again.

"Your father forfeited his right to diplomatic responsibility ten years ago, when he held his brother the prince of Britain to ransom, and used it as an excuse to torment him."

That was true. Medraut had done that. Telemakos had lived for so long in the shadow of his father's love for Lleu that he often conveniently forgot the story of their winter's hunting, and how close they had come to killing each other in rivalry and envy.

Medraut looked directly into the najashi's face and let one cool, accusing word fall from his lips.

"Hypocrite."

Abreha raised two fingers. At the slight movement his servants pulled sharply on the chain that circled Medraut's neck. They held him gasping and speechless until Abreha lowered his hand.

"I gave you fair warning," Abreha said evenly, his black eyes grim beneath his heavy brow.

"What fair warning," Medraut croaked, "to Britain's heir—"

Abreha slashed the air with the edge of his hand, and the men pulled hard on the silencing chain. Medraut's head went back and he plucked at his throat involuntarily.

Muna gripped her husband's arm, and Abreha lowered his hand.

"You were never Britain's heir," Abreha scolded Medraut with quiet intensity.

Medraut, inexplicably, croaked forth one of Grandfather's proverbs in Latin. "'Spiderwebs joined together can catch a lion.'" It sounded strange in Latin, but it made the word *lion* into *leo*, a play on Lleu, the name of the lost prince of Britain.

"Do not make me do this to you, Ras Meder. Do not make your children endure such a spectacle."

Indeed, Athena was gazing intently at the show with wide-eyed interest. Telemakos found himself panicking at the number of terrible things she saw and took for granted. How can I tell anyone anything, like this? It is worse than being in chains myself. Athena shouldn't be here. I wish I wasn't here, either, now. "Hold on to me, Tena," he muttered in her ear. "Both arms around my neck, and hold tight. I'll take you back upstairs to your favorite birds."

She obeyed, but reluctantly. When he tried to climb to his feet she lost her grip, and he could not lift her himself. He bent over her awkwardly, the silver at his elbow making a racket, and tried to get her to put her arms around his neck again, but she was interested in what was going on and would not cooperate.

"Let the Ras do the string stars again," Athena said.

"You can't stay here if the Ras is arguing with the najashi." Telemakos knelt beside her, frustrated and at a loss. "Now listen, Tena, these are your choices . . ." He could not think of any choices to give her. He hesitated, grasping for an ultimatum that would work.

"You may not leave until I have dismissed you, beloved Morningstar," the najashi said. "You are here to show your father your maps."

The najashi turned to Medraut, his heavy frown fierce and forbidding. "Please, Ras Meder. Quit this battle, for your children's sake."

Medraut hesitated. Then he raised his eyebrows doubtfully and repeated, "Morningstar?" His deep voice was full of warmth, despite the cold of his eyes. "Why do you call him Morningstar?"

"Isn't it a good name for him?" Dawit Alta'ir said composedly. With a clean, swift movement of his hands, like an illusionist, he swept the Jacob's ladder from his fingers all at once, and the intricate web disappeared without leaving a single knot. "Athtar, the Morningstar. I named him myself. Prince of the rising generation!"

"Indeed," Medraut said. Then he shook with sudden laughter. "Oh, indeed. Abreha the Federator names him Telemakos the Bright One, and silences me!" He bit his lip and raised a hand quickly, warding off another choking blow. "No need, no need, my lord, I am an obedient guest. Will you allow your guards to slack their hold on me, so I may lean forward? I will hold my tongue. Let Telemakos Morningstar show me his maps."

Telemakos glanced at the najashi, who blinked assent. The soldiers moved aside. Medraut's throat was scored with faint red streaks where the chains had tightened around it, but he showed no sign of the discomfort, only cocked his head to watch as Telemakos set about unrolling the linen sheets.

It was one of a thousand small tasks that gave him no end of trouble. Athena worked attentively at his side so that they could hold down the map together, and Telemakos was glad of the distraction for her sake.

"Here, Ras Meder, is proof of your son's growing store of knowledge," Abreha said. "You'll recognize the map, I think." He drew Athena down into his own lap to keep her out of the way. He reached for the length of string the Star Master had put down and absently began to reconstruct the Jacob's ladder between his own hands. Athena settled comfortably against his chest and pulled at the enticing threads.

"All the beacons in Britain," Medraut observed. "I surely do recognize it. My father's queen drew the original."

He leaned over the chart to study it in concentrated silence. I could have hidden a message there, perhaps, Telemakos thought, if I'd known Ras Meder would see it. I *must* tell him about the plan to attack the Hanish Islands. The najashi hasn't got decent maps yet, and can't get into the fortress, but those agents of his may be in place on the emperor's ships by now—I *must* tell Ras Meder, somehow, before he is sent home.

Medraut spoke at last. "Well done, Telemakos Morning-star," he said warmly. "Your aunt Goewin should see this."

Wild inspiration seized Telemakos.

"Send her my love when you tell her about it," he said.

VIII

GIFTS AND SECRETS

IT WAS THE CODE his mother had instructed him to use in his letters. He was not sure his father would recognize it.

Medraut reached over the map to stop Telemakos's mouth with a warning finger. He spoke softly, and with deliberation, mindful of the chain that was still wound about his neck.

"I'll bear your message to her."

Medraut understood, and was waiting.

Telemakos caught his breath. He was about to launch into the most treacherous perfidy of his life, and he realized it was not fear alone that made him hesitate. Something in the way Athena leaned against the najashi and played the string game with him, so confident and lovingly, made this a cruel and bitter betrayal.

"Athena is like a sandbar in the tide," Telemakos said. He had started now. He drew another breath and went on steadily. "She's like a little island impossible to map, always changing shape and size. You spoke such words yourself, Ras Meder, the day she was born, when you thought I was not listening, *remember*? A little ever-changing island, and the najashi will steal her from you, if you aren't careful. She's surrounded by his children and doesn't know it; she looks at them and speaks their language, thinks they are her own family, and suspects no treachery."

His father watched and listened impassively.

"Look at her, so content and at ease with the federator of Himyar! Your daughter doesn't remember anything of the house of Nebir," Telemakos said, and plunged recklessly further. "Tell our aunt that Athena has forsaken her. She's like a ship with no loyalty, as easily guided by one hand as another. She'll soon be more Himyar than Aksumite."

Medraut's face was quiet, but his dark blue eyes were ablaze.

"You'd better act soon, if you want to keep her," Telemakos said to his father. "Or the najashi and his hunting dogs will win her affection from within."

The najashi seemed absorbed in the game he was playing with Athena, but he surely must be paying close attention to everything Telemakos said. I'd better shut up now, Telemakos thought, or he'll start to wonder why I keep babbling on like this.

"Isn't that so, my najashi?" Telemakos finished, and his uncontrollable voice soared over Abreha's title.

"Aye, I suppose it is," Abreha agreed mildly. "She is my good companion."

Muna touched Athena's springing bronze hair. Athena swatted her hand away absently, then noticed the veil. She reached over the najashi's arm and grabbed and tugged at the sheer silk. "Where's Muna hiding?"

"Perhaps I should take the little princess home with me," Medraut said quietly.

"Sir!" Telemakos gasped in protest. "I meant only—"

Medraut was suddenly intent, with his eyes on his daughter, oblivious to the menace at his throat and the guards at his back.

"Princess."

Athena looked up.

Medraut held out his left palm so that Athena could see the blue serpent and the staff of Asclepius tattooed there. Medraut had used the mark to announce himself as a physician, during the years of silence that had been his private penance for not having died with his brother Lleu in the battle of Camlan. Reaching toward his daughter, he made it seem as if, for a moment, there were a minute, dark dragon nesting in his cupped hand.

Athena ducked beneath the najashi's arm. She dropped lightly to her hands and feet and crawled over to Medraut, intrigued.

Medraut did not move, watching her, still. He closed his hand.

"Gone," Athena said. "See that snake again."

Medraut opened his fingers. His face was expressionless, impassive, immobile as his body.

Athena stood by his side and pointed to the gold dragon that crouched coiled at his shoulder. "Athena see this snake?" she asked politely, careful not to touch without permission.

"Why doesn't she walk yet?" Medraut asked prosaically.

Telemakos was stunned. It had never occurred to him that his father might have the faintest inkling about when a child should normally take her first steps.

"She should be walking," Medraut said. "She's nearly three years old. There's nothing wrong with her legs, is there? Can she stand?"

Medraut took Athena's hand and made her step away from him. She swung against his arm and fell over but pulled herself back up. "Athena see your pretty snake, please, Ras?"

"Can she stand on her own? Will she walk with you if you hold her hands?"

"I can't hold both her hands at once," Telemakos said.

Athena fell over again. She was doing it on purpose. Medraut looked up from her sharply, giving Telemakos a shrewd, assessing glance. "So you can't," he said. "Nor can you lift her anymore."

Telemakos clenched his teeth. He managed to keep his voice even as he said, "Forgive me the contradiction, sir, but if she holds on I can lift her easily."

Medraut deftly unfastened his brooch and, letting the folds of his cloak fall away from his shoulders, tossed the golden dragon across the room. It landed in a cup by the door; his aim was effortless and accurate.

"Go get that, if you want it, little princess. But you must walk to it."

"She does not walk," Muna said.

It was the first she had spoken since they had all come into the room, and Medraut looked at her. She buried her face in her hands beneath the veil.

"My lady," Telemakos said, "Athena is an ungrateful little wretch and does not deserve your attention. She doesn't walk because she's lazy. She knows I'll carry her. It's no blame of yours."

He caught Athena around the waist and hoisted her to her feet again. "Walk a little—come on, Tena, I'll hold your hand."

"Not *Tena*." She sat down contrarily. *"Athena."*

"And you, Telemakos," Medraut said gently. "Your maps are very good. I don't doubt you can draw them from memory. But you can't lift a child or unfold a sheet of cloth. What else? Can you sleep through the night without screaming?"

"Sir—"

But the word came out like the squeal of metal on stone, and Telemakos could not answer.

"Why does he scream in his sleep?" Abreha asked quietly.

Medraut answered with deliberate care. "I took him hunting in the Great Valley of Aksum, two years before he came here, and one day when we had gone separate ways, he was captured by salt traders and taken as a slave to the emperor's salt mines. He was evilly mistreated there, blindfolded and bound, starved, lashed if he stumbled in his work. It was two months before we found him. He still dreams of it. He does not complain of it, though; perhaps he finds it shameful to speak of."

Medraut made it sound so simple: an accident, a mistake, while they should have been hunting together. There was no secret mission, no secret name, no need to hide as Gebre Meskal's sunbird.

"Ai." The najashi gave a sudden sigh, as though surprised by a sharp pain. "I understand now. Beloved Morningstar, I am sorry. I might have spared you a deal of suffering this year, had I known that."

"I'm all right," Telemakos said, embarrassed.

Medraut swallowed again. Telemakos thought he looked tired. He had absorbed the information that could have forfeited both their lives, and turned everyone's attention away from it, and given Telemakos an alibi for his service to the emperor in Afar. And every word he had spoken had been true. It all appeared effortless, but everything he said was calculated to avoid being cut off by the choking chain, and he must surely guess what a razor's edge Telemakos walked himself. When Medraut spoke again, his deep, smooth voice rang with challenge.

"I want *assurance*—" he spoke hesitantly, like a man trying to find his way by throwing his voice in a cavern. "My lord Abreha Anbessa the Lion Hunter, najashi and mukarrib, king of Himyar and federator of South Arabia. Telemakos Meder will not remain in Himyar forever, though you give him another name and raise him in privilege as you would your own children. Give me assurance that he will leave your palace fit for anything his destiny will require of him."

Abreha got up and crossed the room with his purposeful, loping stride. He stopped at the door. "Give me a minute," he said. "I'll make your son a gift, Ras Meder. Wait for me." Then he addressed his soldiers. "I am going to the kennels. It will take me some little time to descend the stairs and come back. Keep the prince silent while I'm gone."

Medraut sat taut and motionless, an alabaster statue, with his hands on his knees. After a few moments, when no one moved or said anything, Athena got to her hands and feet and crawled over to the cup where Medraut had thrown his dragon brooch. She pulled herself up to stand at the table and, with a glance over her shoulder to make sure she was not doing anything wrong, tipped up the cup and fished out the pin. She scrambled back to Telemakos on three feet—or anyway on her feet and one hand—holding the dragon carefully in her other hand. Then she sat contentedly to examine it.

Dawit spoke suddenly again. "Before Medraut courted your mother, boy, he courted my daughter Muna."

"*Sir!*" Queen Muna cried out.

Dawit sniffed. "It was not secret then. Why should it be secret now you are both married, and not to each other?"

Whatever Telemakos had expected the najashi to be hiding from him, it was not this. He felt as though he had been standing by a dark window, and now a curtain was pulled back so that he could see through to another world, full of a new kind of intrigue that it never occurred to him to watch for.

Medraut's eyes seethed. He did not move or make a sound.

"There is your reason the najashi did not want Gwalchmei as his ambassador, Morningstar," Dawit added. "He looks too much like his cousin, your father, and lacked your father's temperance. Gwalchmei was a captivating libertine."

"Do not shame me," Muna said quietly.

"Hah!" Dawit grunted. "The boy is the image of his father. Do you think the najashi will allow him to stay in this palace after his voice breaks?"

When the najashi returned to the room, there were two young salukis pressed close against his legs. Medraut smacked his thigh hard with his fist as a wordless exclamation and broke into a real smile of surprise and delight. Again Athena scrambled to the door on all fours, lionlike. She pulled herself up against the belly of a saluki. The dog turned its head nervously and sniffed at her. "Mine," Athena said. "Athena's dog, thank you, najashi."

That made even the guards' mouths twitch. Medraut laughed aloud.

"I am sorry, my honey badger," the najashi apologized, getting down on her level as he always did to talk to children. "But these dogs are for your brother. I am sure he will share them."

Now Telemakos was completely mystified. He stared at his guardian in frozen disbelief.

"For *me?*" He was sure the najashi meant some mockery or jest.

"Aye, for you, Morningstar. Your father bids me give him assurance of my good intent toward you, and we all know you could use assistance in the hunt. These will be easier for you to manage than a falcon."

Telemakos's mind raced. A pair of hunting dogs? A *pair!* Two of the najashi's gazelle hounds for my own? The last one he gave away was a gift for the emperor of Aksum. What is going on?

They were a matched pair, an identical hound and bitch, not a year old and not quite full grown. Their legs and bodies were the pearly golden white of old ivory, or new cream, or Telemakos's own pale hair. Their long, silken ears and feathery tails were red as copper.

"You cannot possibly . . ." Telemakos moved to kneel formally before Abreha, with his head turned aside in disbelief as much as humility, and muttered, "My lord najashi, this is a gift for a king. I do not deserve this." He drew a shaking breath, burning with shame at having to accept such a gift bare minutes after attempting something close to treason. "Never in a thousand years would I deserve such dogs."

"I do not doubt that you are right on both counts," Abreha replied dryly. "But they are yours. My gift to you is my pledge to your father."

Medraut answered him with real warmth and fervor. "Truly,

my najashi, you do my son a great honor to gift him so generously. You do us both a great honor. I accept this pledge."

The najashi strode across the room to join Medraut where
he sat. The dogs followed loyally at his heels.

"Touch them, Morningstar. Let them smell you. You are
their master now."

Telemakos had always known he would sell his soul to call
one of these dogs his own. He could not restrain himself for
one second longer, and his lips were against their feathery copper ears while his roughened fingertips snagged the white silk
of their coats. They warmed to the game joyfully, sniffing and
butting their heads against him, so that for a moment he forgot
everything else.

"Oh, my najashi, *thank you!*" Telemakos gasped.

Athena was as enraptured as he was.

"Mine, Boy, Tena's pretty dog," she argued with him. "Selene, Selene."

Telemakos laughed. "All right, then, Selene! Selene and
Argos! You may share, you selfish thing."

Does this mean I'm safe? Telemakos wondered, and in
his mind felt again the light sting of parchment striking his
cheek.

It doesn't, he decided. The najashi will never trust me. But
it is an apology, a payment for that terrible season of discipline
and hardship he made me endure.

Overcome with conflicting emotions, Telemakos suddenly
threw himself at Medraut and hid his face against his father's

shoulder. He felt Medraut's arms tighten around him like steel bands. He had never known fear in that harsh embrace, never anything but trust and safety. But Medraut, too, could be merciless. He had whipped Athena's fingers with strips of hide when, at less than a year old, she had interfered with the sling he was braiding. He had held a knife to his young brother's throat.

The charm bracelet chattered. Telemakos raised his head. His eyes burned, but he had managed not to weep.

"Give my love to Goewin," Telemakos reminded Medraut.

IX

Marib

HE WAS IN a foul mood in the weeks following his father's visit: one day, that one day being all they had had. It had not even been a day, really, just those few hours in the najashi's reception room, with Medraut held in chains the whole of their time together.

So the najashi kept his promise and took Telemakos to see the dam at Marib. The journey, Telemakos knew, was meant to console and distract him, and he resisted consolation. But it worked anyway. Telemakos liked traveling. He liked being part of a royal retinue; it was on one of Gebre Meskal's hunting parties that Telemakos had first met Abreha, when the najashi had come to Aksum to witness Gebre Meskal's initiation as emperor. The journey Abreha made to Marib now was a routine check on the dam and the dedication of a monument commemorating its rebuilding. But the najashi traveled with all the trappings of an imperial progress, including his wife and his gazelle hounds and Malika the child queen of Sheba, who was heir to the Marib principality. When the silk tents were raised in Marib's green fields, it felt like a party.

Athena did not like Marib. The empty windows of the ruined palace there scared her, as did the dark, abandoned pre-Christian temple that was half buried beneath drifting sand. All around the great dam, and the irrigated land that it watered, orange groves stretched so far out on the plains toward the desert that you could not see their borders. But you could not get rid of the sand that blew in from the desert reaches of the Empty Quarter. When the wind blew, Athena rode at Telemakos's side with her face hidden in his shoulder, or with a length of his shamma pulled over her head, to keep the sand out of her eyes. She spat with vicious disdain when it got in her mouth; you had to filter water before you could drink it. City children were paid to sweep the sand away from the buttresses around the great dam's sluices.

But Telemakos liked Marib. In part he was honestly impressed at the work Abreha had done here, restoring a piece of engineering a thousand years old, with such painstaking attention that a land of semi-desert was transformed into a green valley that could produce grain throughout the year. And in part Telemakos was simply glad to be out of San'a, and the endless stairways of the Ghumdan palaces.

Telemakos and Athena, and the young salukis Argos and Selene, slept outside the tents on still nights. The tail end of winter was passing; the dry, sandy soil still kept the day's heat and was warm to the touch throughout the evening. Weaverbirds nested where the grass grew long and insects sang. The wind died after sundown, and you could breathe again without getting sand up your nose. Lines of ancient willow trees radiated outward from the dam, showing where the oldest of the water courses had run, buried now but still nourishing the trees. The warriors and courtiers sat with their dogs beneath the trailing leaves, telling stories and laughing in the dark. Telemakos liked to listen. It was easy to listen to the warriors' storytelling, and safe.

And he liked the hunting. The najashi had his own hunting grounds here, as well as the right to the wilderness afforded by the principality, and rather than slaughter the local livestock for his retinue, Abreha allowed his men to hunt for themselves. The najashi ran Menelik with the salukis in daily chases across the highland plains. The lion even killed an oryx, which he slunk away from obediently when told to; Menelik was fully grown now, if not as heavy as Solomon had been. Telemakos was happy to let Abreha take mastery over the lion in the hunt, for it left him free to concentrate on his young dogs or his javelins.

He was able to manage the short spears well now, two strapped to his back and a third balanced lightly across his thighs if he was riding, or tilted over his shoulder if he was on foot. Liberated from the exacting work of keeping Menelik in check, Telemakos brought down a splendid ibex, his first kill since before his accident. The great, curved horns were taller than Athena.

"Those will ward off evil and bring rain," Abreha told Telemakos. "So say our tribesmen. What will you do with such useful talismans?"

"May I send them to my father?"

"May I suggest you send them to Constantine, the high king of Britain?" Abreha said. "Your fatherland is in need of rain. It will make a good impression, and you may send your next trophy to your father."

Telemakos sighed inwardly; there was no point in arguing if the najashi already had a plan thought out for him. Constantine the high king of Britain was possibly the last person Telemakos would have thought of to honor with a hunting trophy, but he could see the diplomatic sense in the gesture. "Of course," he murmured judiciously.

The gazelle hounds Argos and Selene came with Telemakos when he hunted. Selene glued herself to his left side, whether or not he was carrying Athena on his hip; the saluki seemed to know by instinct that this was the side of him that lay defenseless. Selene was already intensely loyal, Telemakos knew, to Athena as much as to himself, and would have died to defend either one of them.

He had to fight Athena for possession of the dogs. She screamed and threw a tantrum every time he took them hunting, though sometimes it was just because she wanted to come along, or did not want to leave Telemakos. She would let Muna carry her now, but very few other people. Apart from Telemakos, the najashi was still her favorite. He let her ride on the lion's back whenever he took her walking around Marib. Her world was so strange Telemakos despaired of her ever becoming reasonable.

"Your choices are: let go of Selene's neck *now*, or you may not play with her when I get back from the hunt."

Athena let go. The dogs were the only thing that made her behave.

The formal dedication of the monument was approaching, but work on the dam continued, and the najashi postponed his return to San'a until the gathering of the Great Assembly. That gave them a full dry season in Marib.

One afternoon, the najashi and his retainers went prowling up the great wadi valley that delivered water to the ancient drainage system above the dam. As the land grew harsher and drier and willow gave way to acacia, the salukis came upon a spoor that excited them. "That's a male lion, and a big one," said Tharan, looking up from the tracks.

Telemakos knelt beside him. "There're two." The lions were padding in parade, one behind the other. "Look here—they passed this way within minutes of us, and marked this place— can you smell it? They're marking their territory, not hunting."

"Two lions prowling this close to the city!" exclaimed Tharan.

"Worse than vermin," agreed Alim the local governor, Malika's uncle, who came along as their guide. "Chase them for sport, if you like, Abreha the Lion Hunter. Otherwise it will be a job for the city guard to kill them or drive them off."

Hunting together, the najashi's gazelle hounds were said to have taken lions, Telemakos knew. He stood trying to quell his excitement. He had not hunted lions before; at least, not looking for a fight, not with a sharpened spear to call his own, and not with anyone's permission.

"Will you lead us, Morningstar?" Abreha requested decisively, as though it were a formality, as though there were no one else to ask.

Telemakos's heart vaulted with gratitude and excitement. "My najashi, of course."

"Stand steady."

Abreha refixed the scarf that muffled Telemakos's charm bracelet, and reached to Tharan, who handed him one of the light spears for Telemakos to take.

"You are better balanced holding a lance. Are those on your back in readiness? Good. Lead on."

Telemakos held his head up for a few moments, gauging the wind. He breathed deep and choked on sand. He put down the spear for a moment, and kneeling with the neck of his shirt pulled up over his nose, took another deep breath. He was trying to catch the lingering trace of the lions' bodies beyond the stink of cat that they had left about; but Menelik padded at the najashi's side, and the only scent Telemakos could make out was Menelik's familiar smell of oil and honey.

It's *this*, he thought, his mouth dry and his pulse begin-ning to race. I love this. This is my favorite part of the hunt, the tracking, the finding. The kill is nothing to the chase, nothing. If I had never to do anything else but this, I would be happy.

He picked up his spear and set out in the direction pointed by the tracks, falling into a light jog that he could easily check when he needed to confirm the trail. Argos and Selene trotted one on either side of him, and the najashi's host followed be-hind. It was not the first time the najashi had let him lead them in their tracking; Telemakos could scent the quarry nearly as well as the dogs and was better at reporting it.

They overtook the lions high in a barren gully carved by years of seasonal rains. Telemakos fell back and let the hounds close in. A dozen of them concentrated their effort on the small-er of the lions, and overwhelmed it, though it put up a furious fight; its heavier companion came snarling to its defense from outside the fray. The bigger lion killed a saluki in one single snap of its jaws, crushing the back of the slender creature's head and neck. One of the men let out a cry of sorrow then, and the huntsmen waded in among the dogs with their spears. The defending lion turned tail and leaped silently away among the rocks, trailing blood.

"It's taken a spear thrust in the thigh," someone called. "It won't get far."

Telemakos heard Abreha give a command, in his gentle speaking-to-the-hounds voice. "Go, my beauty. Take him." In a flash of tawny gold and black, Menelik loped after the vanished lion.

That thing is a quarter again Menelik's size, Telemakos thought in alarm, and enraged with a superficial wound.

He ran. He leaped up the gully as lightly and nearly as swiftly as the young lion, leveling himself with the short spear, but he was not quick enough to stop the fight before it started. Menelik and the wild lion were going at each other with abandon when Telemakos arrived. They snapped and bellowed, rolling and whipping their bodies in the sand with such lightning speed Telemakos could not follow their fight.

"Menelik! *Menelik! Hold!*"

What Telemakos did next he did without thinking. He gripped his short spear tight against his ribs and launched himself at the lions.

The wild one took its teeth out of Menelik's neck and lunged toward Telemakos; its own momentum carried it right into his spear. Telemakos held the lance fast and thrust it straight back through the lion's open mouth and down the growling throat. Selene went for its throat also, and clung there with her jaws locked shut, relentless and determined as a mosquito. As the lion fell at his feet, Telemakos hauled his second spear out of its brace, over his back, and threw all his weight into a final blow between the lion's shoulders. He could feel the blade grinding against that of his first spear as he drove them together inside the terrible neck.

Selene still held on. Telemakos, too, held himself there for a moment, bent over and panting, half expecting the lion to leap up again and devour him. When nothing happened, he dared to look up. Menelik lay choking on blood that streamed from his mouth and nostrils. The wild lion had torn out his throat.

For a few moments more Telemakos stood still, knowing he could give Menelik neither help nor any comfort. Then, in bitter grief and fury, he braced himself with his foot against the carcass of the lion he had just killed, wrenched free the spear in its back, and drove it between Menelik's ribs, through his heart.

"Morningstar!" The rest of the hunters had caught up with him. "Hai! Morningstar! Are you hurt?"

"What's the boy done? *Mother of God!*"

Men lifted Telemakos away from the dead animals. There was jubilation in their gibbering voices. He found himself standing before Abreha, who held open arms to him; Telemakos never afterward knew whether Abreha meant to congratulate him or to comfort him. He had no chance to do either: Telemakos flew at him and slapped him across the face.

"Lion against lion!"

Telemakos's voice cracked, sounding as babyish as Athena's in his own ears.

"Against his own kind! A *lion* against his own kind! You would not set a dog against another dog, oh never, not one of your precious salukis, but you would so despise a *lion?*"

The huntsmen had fallen silent now.

"And not one of your guard had wit enough to stop it happening! Ah, God, I am ashamed to be gifted with your damned dogs. Give me next time a pair of songbirds, so I won't have to be party to another such *murder!*"

"Quiet, child, calm yourself," Abreha said. "Calm yourself."

Telemakos screamed at him, *"What am I going to tell Athena?"* He burst into tears.

They tried to make him drink water that was bitter with the taste of some added sedative. Telemakos spat this out in fury and struck the man who had offered him the drinking horn. They pinned Telemakos by the shoulders while Tharan pinched his nose shut until he gasped for breath. When Telemakos opened his mouth, Tharan jerked his head back in one swift movement and poured the drink straight down his throat.

"You are a damned pack of hyenas!" Telemakos wept, spitting and coughing. Abreha caught him gently when he fell.

He was lying on his back beneath the willows. Stars appeared and disappeared above him through the shifting leaves. Athena slept with her arms around his neck and her head against his shoulder, a warm, affectionate bundle of banked energy pressing him against the ground. The salukis were curled beside him as well, one tight against each leg. One of them had its head propped on his stomach.

He was still immobilized by the sedative and battled for

consciousness. Someone else was there, someone awake, touching his head: combing his hair, so gently and lightly it did not hurt, even when the quick hands pulled through the snarls.

"He doesn't like being put to sleep," Muna said. "His father spends more on opium for him than the Scions are allowed for their clothes, and he disdains it. Rasha has found unopened vials of the stuff tied in his shirttails. You should not force it on him, even to calm him. You deal harshly with him, my lord."

She was picking the sand from Telemakos's scalp and plaiting his hair in tight rows against his skull, in the neat style of the Himyar warriors. He knew that she was using clarified butter to oil his hair, because he recognized the smell, but he could not remember where he was or why he had been drugged. It was all right; Athena was there.

"I dare not spoil him with any softness," murmured the najashi's voice. "For a prince of his stature, he is flawed severely enough as it is. Old enough to train as a warrior, and afraid to sleep alone! I hoped the dogs would come to substitute for the child as his comforter. Why should he need anything at all, this half-grown youth who killed two lions today all unaided? In Aksum, in my homeland, killing a lion is the ritual test of a king. If you can kill a lion, you are deemed fit to rule a kingdom."

"He can't light a lamp," said Muna. "He can't comb his hair. He can't drink from a waterskin. He can't sharpen his pens. He is healing, only healing still, and you deal harshly with him."

"He has slain a *lion*," the najashi said. "He could kill a man. He shouldn't need help with lamps and combs! He *doesn't* need it, any more than his sister needs to be carried about like a lap dog. She's three years old. When will she learn to walk?" He sighed. "Neither one of them is whole. Neither one of them sleeps peacefully without the other near."

They talk about us as though we were their own children, Telemakos thought, and fell back into his drugged sleep.

He woke again shortly after dawn, still unable to govern his body, and found himself trapped in the illusion of imprisonment that had scarred his mind in Afar. If he tried to move his legs, they were chained. If he tried to move his arms, they were bound. If he tried to open his eyes, they were held shut by the dreaded, hated blindfold. He struggled until he began to weep aloud. And then out of nowhere the najashi was holding him, clasping him firmly hand in hand and stroking his hair.

After a little while Telemakos murmured unhappily, "You must hate it that I am alive and your son Asad is not. I think that is why you are so strict with me."

"I was not strict enough with Asad," the najashi answered gently. "He had neither your will nor your endurance. God forbid you should grow to be so soft and submissive. Your aunt Goewin took him for a servant the one time she met him."

"I am soft. I am a coward. I am always so afraid, sleeping and waking, it never gets any easier, any less cruel, any lighter. I am always so *afraid!*"

"So are we all," Abreha said. "You learn to master it. Or you pay it no heed, as a lion pays no heed to the dangers of the life he leads. He lives from kill to kill, from drought to drought, from pride to pride. What safety is there in his life? He is always afraid, and never knows it. It does not ruin him."

"Where is Athena?"

"Breaking her fast with my queen, like a good girl."

"I want my dogs, then," Telemakos said.

"They're here."

Telemakos had not noticed them, lying against him.

"Master it," Abreha repeated. "Do not be afraid."

Telemakos spent the morning watching the men working over the hide of his golden lion. The lions he had known in the highlands of Aksum were black maned, but this one that he killed in Himyar was all over a molten, burnished gold, from mane to tail. He could not believe how big it was. Its skin was bigger than the one that hung in Kidane's reception hall at home, which Medraut had caught for Turunesh before Telemakos was born.

"What will your father say to *this* trophy when he receives it?" Abreha asked him, and laughed at his own question. "He'll forbid you to go hunting again, most likely, in case you damage yourself." Then the najashi added, more soberly, "The other hide is yours as well."

"I don't want it."

"Send it to your aunt."

I could do that, Telemakos thought; no one has ever given Goewin such a trophy of her own. She'll be pleased. And she will understand why I've done it.

They did not tell Athena what had happened. They sent Menelik's skin to Aksum and hoped she would not notice that her lion was gone.

X

THE TREE OF KNOWLEDGE

THEY ARRIVED BACK in San'a as the nobles began to gather for the Great Assembly. Two years ago, they had been gathering for the Assembly when Telemakos had first arrived in Himyar, and again during his disgrace of the previous year. This year's gathering was the third he would witness. Some of the Scions would sit in on the Assembly this year.

On the evening they came back to the Ghumdan palaces, Telemakos found the star globe alight in the Great Globe Room. He sat on his low bed by the window and let Athena unbuckle the straps to her harness so she could climb out of it. "Look how the Magus has welcomed us home," Telemakos said softly. Dawit could no longer see the soft lights the globe's pinprick surface cast against the ceiling; he never lit it for any reason other than to delight Athena.

Everything else in the room was exactly as Telemakos had

left it a season earlier. The neglect was almost eerie. Dawit Alta'ir had touched nothing here for three months. A film of dust lay over the maps and measures; a cup of paint that Telemakos had left sitting on one of the windowsills still sat there, dry as mortar. He set about the renovation of his workplace, moving around the room on his knees; he was so tall now that he had to dodge the hanging crystal stars if he walked upright among them. He worked by the minute lights of the star globe. Athena sat very quietly on the couch, happily sorting the paint blocks she had not played with since the beginning of summer.

It gave Telemakos a start when Dawit suddenly appeared in the doorway. He carried no light, and came heavily down the three steps into the room. The scent of rosewater and kat came with him.

"Peace to you, Magus," Telemakos greeted the Star Master, but Dawit did not sit. He reached up and took hold of one of the crystal stars, as if it would bear his weight if he lost his balance. Telemakos identified the star automatically: Antares, the heart of the Scorpion.

"Peace to you, Morningstar. Good evening, and welcome back to San'a. I wonder if in your travels you've missed the news from Adulis, where Gebre Meskal stations most of his armada?"

"What news?"

"There has been a battle, and a great mutiny suppressed."

"Oh."

Telemakos still held a rolled map, which he had been about to put away. He laid it gently on the floor.

"Fifty soldiers of the najashi's who served in a squadron of Gebre Meskal's fleet were attacked and overwhelmed. They are prisoners now."

"Oh," Telemakos said again, sounding stupid now even to himself. He clenched his teeth and made himself form a sensible response. "What does this mean, sir?"

"It means the najashi would like to ask you some questions," said Dawit evenly, "though why you should know anything about a mutiny on the far side of the Red Sea is anyone's guess. So. Consider that I have given you fair warning, and answer me: did you know of this before our najashi knew of it?"

"*How could I?*" Telemakos gasped.

"Good," said Dawit. "I thought you couldn't, as you were away in Marib at the time."

The old, sickening fear crawled up and down Telemakos's spine.

"Is he coming up here now?"

"He is waiting in the scriptorium. He wants to speak to you privately. I will send him in."

The Star Master gathered his robes about his knees and heaved himself back up the steps. Telemakos sat where he was. He picked up the map again, but he was shaking so that the charms at his elbow rattled. He set the scroll down again and waited with his eyes closed.

"The Magus didn't see me," said Athena.

Telemakos had forgotten she was there.

"He can't see," Telemakos said softly. "And it's quite dark."

"The najashi has got a light."

Telemakos opened his eyes. He watched the light grow brighter until the najashi's shadow filled the door. Abreha came in and put his lamp on the floor, then sat down facing Telemakos and held out his arm to Athena.

She slid from the mattress and scuttled on hands and feet to join him. The lights in the dark surface of the star globe glowed steadily overhead.

"Look at the stars, my najashi!"

"They're lovely, my honey badger." He smoothed her springing hair back from her face. "Be quiet now, and sit with me. I want to talk to your brother."

Telemakos sat back on his heels and bowed his head. A part of him wanted to scream at Abreha to get this over with; Telemakos had been living in dread of this conversation, or one like it, for well over a year. But Abreha did not hurry. He pulled Athena close to him, with her back against his chest. One hand he wrapped about her waist, and the other he held circling her throat, gently, gently cupping her chin.

Telemakos found himself gripping his own shoulder. He heard the trinkets of his bracelet clinking as he clenched and unclenched his fingers, and for a moment tried solely to concentrate on being still.

The najashi bent his heavy brow and spoke softly into the bronze mist of Athena's hair.

"My honey badger, I want you to ask your brother a question for me. Can you do this?"

She gazed at Telemakos with wide, wondering eyes.

"Ask the boy who sent him here."

She demanded obediently, "Who sent you here?"

Telemakos raised his head. The silver bells rang wildly.

"Who sent you?" the beloved, childish voice insisted.

"My grandfather sent me," Telemakos hissed, "for my protection; as you know, my najashi."

The najashi murmured again in Athena's ear. "Ask the boy if he told my cousin where to find my men."

She repeated in her deep, clear baby voice, "Did you tell his cousin where his friends are?"

Telemakos could not answer.

"You knew," the najashi said quietly. "You knew, and you wanted Gebre Meskal to know. Did you tell him in a letter?" He wrapped his arms around Athena's neck and waist, like a gentle python tightening its coils. "Try to copy exactly what I say, little honey badger. Ask the boy, 'Are you employed by the emperor Gebre Meskal?'"

She blinked in agreement. "Are you employed by the emperor Gebre Meskal?"

Telemakos hid his face in the crook of his elbow. The charms brushed cold against his cheek and chin.

"Are you employed by the emperor?" his baby sister asked again, patiently.

"I have not formally sworn allegiance to anyone!" Telemakos cried aloud, his face hidden.

"Good girl," the king murmured at Athena's ear. "The boy knows as much and more about Gebre Meskal's kingdom as he does about mine. I'll wager he knows secrets I have spent years in trying to discover. He does not want to tell me, my honey badger, but I think he will tell you. Ask him . . ." He whispered at her ear again. Now the najashi's strong, narrow fingers were locked around her throat.

She said, "Who is the sunbird?"

The words took Telemakos like a blow to the stomach, knocking the breath from his chest.

"Who is the sunbird?"

And with the iron hands poised ready to snap his sister's neck, all Telemakos's resolution evaporated. He was damned now.

"Who is the sunbird?"

"I am," he whispered.

The najashi breathed out a sudden, shaking sigh, like a soft explosion. He said, as though it were absurd, "The informer that stopped all Aksum's exports of salt during the plague quarantine? The sunbird? The *sunbird?*"

"You have said so," Telemakos whispered.

"You were no more than a child during Gebre Meskal's quarantine!"

"I have no authority," Telemakos acknowledged, speaking

through his teeth. "But I hear everything. What do you imagine I was doing, hunting on my own in the Salt Desert, four years ago? My father made it sound like an accident when he told you. But I did it knowingly, I did it on purpose, I thought out the plan myself! I crossed Afar on foot, and then sold myself into servitude so that I might find out the identity of your captain there—" It was wonderful to be damned. You did not have to guard yourself at all. "—Anako archon of Deire, who held me captive and gave the order that my fingernails be torn out and salt splinters be rubbed into my eyes, not knowing who I was! I owed you no loyalty whatever in Afar!"

"You owe it to me now," the najashi said simply. He whispered again in Athena's ear. She parroted his words calmly.

"The najashi reminds you of—what is the word, najashi?"

She waited, listening attentively. Then she spoke again, pleased to be doing this challenging work so well.

"The najashi reminds you of your covenant with him."

Abreha the Lion Hunter raised his head, let go of Athena's throat, and reached toward Telemakos. Telemakos pulled away from him. The silver bracelet crashed and clattered.

Telemakos began, "I swear, I swear by my life—"

The Lion Hunter interrupted contemptuously, "What is your life worth?"

Telemakos swallowed. "By my sister's life, then. My grandfather thought the threats Gedar delivered to our house, the murdered sunbirds, were meant for me. We didn't know you suspected my father, or my grandfather, or whomever body it was you were trying to flush out for getting in the way of your cursed salt smuggling! I was sent here for my own protection, and not to cast abroad the secrets of your kingdom!"

"Then deny that you have done so."

Telemakos knelt bent double with his face hidden in the crook of his arm, and could not answer. The silver charms scratched his cheek.

"Deny that you have done so, knowing full well what the consequence would be should I discover you."

Telemakos thought he heard the najashi set Athena on the floor, but he could not summon the strength to raise his head and look.

"'Of the tree of the knowledge of good and evil you shall not eat,'" the najashi said, "'for in the day you eat of it you shall die.'" His voice was not so steady as it had been. "I want to treat you justly, Morningstar. And, God help me, I want desperately to forgive you. But it is not me alone you have betrayed: it is my *kingdom*, my nation, my people."

Telemakos raised his head at last, his eyes burning, unable to endure such hypocrisy.

"You are *Aksumite*," he said, "and these are *not your people*."

Abreha spoke to Telemakos in deadly quiet, his upper lip curled in scorn.

"Mother of God, you shame yourself."

The baby was still sitting on his lap, but now the najashi did lift her to the floor. She stayed leaning quietly against his knee, sensing that she had not entirely been dismissed.

"I never thought to hear such narrow, blind intolerance from you, you of all, *you*, who have your mother's African skin and your father's North Sea eyes. You are blood kin to my dead children. Do you deny your great-uncle the Star Master? Do you wash yourself of Sheba and Qataban, whose future sovereigns adore you? You call yourself Aksumite; do you bear no allegiance to Goewin of Britain? Who are *your* people, Athtar, Lij Bitwoded Telemakos Eosphorus?"

The najashi picked up his lamp and stood up. "You shame yourself," he repeated quietly. "You are justly condemned. I shall leave my guard outside your door, as befits an arrested traitor awaiting sentence. But they will not disturb you. Put your sister to bed now."

He turned back at the top of the steps.

"I never sent a single one of your letters home," he told Telemakos. "I could not see your hidden treachery, but you are trickier than a hunted lizard, and I knew it must be lurking there somewhere. I thought to spare you the fault of sending them, so I burned each one as soon as you left my study. Gebre Meskal discovered my plans on his own."

The najashi took a deep breath, and added bitterly, "Nor would I *ever* harm that child beside you, though you knew all the secrets of Rome and Persia, and I thought I could get it out of you by plucking one hair from her head. You are thwarted by your own guilty conscience."

He closed the door heavily behind him.

Telemakos knelt staring at his sister without seeing her. His treachery was real, even if his letters had not been sent. He had spoken aloud the information that damned him now, in the coded message to Goewin he had given his father.

Athena pulled herself to her feet, holding on to his shirt.

"The najashi did tell me what to say," she pointed out.

"You did well, Tena," Telemakos whispered.

"Not Tena. *Athena*."

"Athena. You did well, Athena."

He hugged her close against him and buried his face in her hair. The sandalwood scent was nearly gone; it had been her baby smell. She was different now, trying so hard to be grown up. She changed so quickly.

I will never see her walk, now, Telemakos thought; nor hear her say my name.

"Little Tena," Telemakos whispered, spilling hot, silent tears into her neck. "I mean, Athena. Oh, my sister . . ." He clutched her close against him, choking with grief: not because he faced losing his life, but because he faced losing her.

Will he make it a public execution, like the one we saw in al-Muza? Telemakos wondered. Will Athena have to *see*? What will they tell her has happened to me? What will they do with her after?

He thought, I must get her away from me before it happens. I have got to let her go.

"Athena," he choked quietly, speaking into her neck. "I'm going to go away. You may not see me again after tonight . . ."

"Boy?" she said uncertainly.

He made her sit so that they were face-to-face in the dark, and tried to be as serious and as clear as he was able. "You won't see me again. Just as you won't see Menelik again. You must kiss me good-bye now, and after this you have got to learn to walk by yourself, and behave for Muna and the najashi and the others who will take care of you—not like last time, when you set fire to the trees and made messes everywhere."

He could feel her shoulders fall. Her whole frame seemed to crumple, and she began to sob.

"I will try to send you home to our mother, Turunesh, and to Ras Meder. You remember Ras Meder, with the snake in his hand?"

She cried tragically. She stood against his shoulder with her smooth brown arms around his neck and wept. "I do not want Ras Meder! I want to be with you!"

He held her close, his eyes closed, unable to speak.

Then she sat down. She grabbed the parchment map at his side and beat it against the ground and tore at it with her teeth. She threw it across the room and screamed in fury, "I am *not* good! I *will* make a mess! I will bite them and hit them and throw the rice again, I do *not* want to see you *pinned up on a stick like the lion with blood on your feet! That* is what they did with the lion, I saw it, the najashi did *lie* to me when he told me it went away, and I will *not be good!*"

She threw herself at Telemakos again and clutched him

around the neck frantically. "Stay with *Athena*, Boy," she sobbed. "Stay with me."

Telemakos whispered numbly, "I can't."

It was true; that was what had happened to Menelik's skin, before it went to Goewin. Athena must have seen it and said nothing. What else did she know; what else did she see?

Telemakos sat in the dark, clinging to her while she heaved with angry sobs, and after a time, through the chill that seemed to have taken hold of his mind, an idea came to him.

"Listen, Athena," Telemakos whispered. "If you promise to be good, and to eat your food nicely and let Muna get you dressed and washed, and try to walk instead of being carried all the time, I will give you my salukis."

"I don't want *dogs*. I want *you*."

"I won't be here. Listen, Athena, these are your choices. You can have the dogs and be good, or you can have no dogs and be wretched. Which do you choose?"

"I don't want dogs!"

"You get to choose dogs or nothing."

She burst into tears again. He held her on his lap, his own tears making her hair wet, but then she finally made up her mind, sobbing in the pitiful way she did when she felt sorry for herself. "I will have the dogs then, and walk by myself, and not bite Muna. Is it all right if I am crying, Boy? Will I have the dogs if I'm crying? I don't know how to make my eyes stop."

"It's all right if you cry," Telemakos said softly. "Muna does not mind children crying. She'll understand. The Scions will understand, too."

For though they did not often speak of their own lost parents, their dead sisters and brothers, grief was a crippling wound suffered by all Abreha's foster children.

He let her curl against his side with one hand in his hair to go to sleep, as usual. Telemakos lay still and quiet until her small, smooth fingers fell away, relaxed, and she was unlikely to wake again soon.

"My lovely, bold Athena." He kissed her on the forehead. "Sleep well, my sister, my goddess."

She growled to herself in her sleep, dreaming about her salukis.

Telemakos stood up and stripped off his shirt. The noble chieftains of his homeland in Aksum would often come before their sovereign naked to the waist if they had a favor to beg; the gesture would not be lost on the najashi.

Telemakos left Athena sleeping under the false stars and lowered himself through the pulley hole.

He swung for a moment by his fingertips before dropping to the floor of the nursery with a thump and a jangle. Lu'lu sat up, looked at him, then lay back down and turned over to go back to sleep. Telemakos recovered himself and went through to the children's room. The seven eldest of the Scions were sitting in a circle playing Honest Man, Thief.

"How did you get in here, Morningstar?" Malika said.

"Come and join the game. We need a vizier; every roll of the bone turns up another soldier, and no one has had any tasks set them yet."

"I can't. I—"

They waited, all looking up at him expectantly.

"I am in disgrace again," he said, his voice scarcely more than a whisper.

Their gasp of sorrow and disbelief came out in unison, and again Telemakos was so griefstruck that for one blind moment he could not breathe.

"What may we do?" Inas asked in a low voice. "We will do anything we can."

"Thank you," Telemakos said. "Don't tell anyone you've seen me."

They watched in silence as he crossed the room beneath the bone and silver birdcages.

"We are with you," Shadi and Jibril said to his departing back.

"We are all with you," Inas echoed.

Telemakos no longer needed to muffle the charms at his elbow if he wanted to move in silence. He made his way through Ghumdan's marble corridors and no one heard him; no one saw him.

The najashi's own guards, outside Abreha's apartment, were chatting together in normal, relaxed voices. Telemakos came as close as he could without actually touching them and took bitter pleasure in surprising one of them into dropping his spear.

"The najashi said I can speak to him whenever I want," Telemakos muttered petulantly, falling to his knees with a deliberate and satisfying commotion of tinsel. The soldier snatched up the spear and pressed it against Telemakos's bare ribs, and the other held a long knife at his throat. Telemakos was determined to make them feel like a pair of idiots. He shrank from the steel and scrubbed at his nose as if he were trying not to cry. He let the bells at his elbow plink and prattle.

"How—"

The soldiers gave each other quick, accusatory glances.

"Didn't you hear him?"

Telemakos bowed his head. "Please don't hurt me. The najashi is expecting me." He shook the charms again. "I startle people everywhere I go," he sniffed. "I'm sorry."

They lowered their weapons. Telemakos was sure he looked pathetically harmless, a frightened, one-armed boy wearing only a kilt. But all the palace knew he had slain two lions, unaided, in the past season. The guards glanced at each other uneasily.

"Stay with him," said the spearman. "I'll step within."

He did, and after a few moments, beyond the door and the silken arras that covered it, Telemakos heard the murmur of voices. He waited, and soon Muna came into the hall. Her own bracelets chittered. She wore an astonishing surcoat figured with pomegranates, each fruit outlined with gold thread and seeded with what looked like real rubies. For a long moment she said nothing but stood quietly, gazing down at Telemakos kneeling there; then she knelt beside him with her palm laid gently on his good shoulder.

"Morningstar, it is late."

"I seek a petition of the najashi," Telemakos said.

"Does the Star Master know you're here? Did he send you?"

She means, did he let me past the guards, Telemakos thought. So she knows I am in disgrace again.

Telemakos whispered, *"No one sent me."*

Muna's hand trembled against his cold skin like a leaf in the wind tugging at its stem. Telemakos glanced up at her through his lashes. She met his gaze for a moment, as she had done on his first night in San'a.

"I would speak with the najashi," Telemakos repeated.

"Come in, then," Muna said, raising him to his feet. Telemakos was taller than she was. "My husband is still at his desk." She led Telemakos through her chambers without taking her hand from his shoulder, until she left him alone so that she might forewarn the najashi. After a short while she came back and wordlessly waved Telemakos within.

XI

THE SEALED AGREEMENT

THERE WAS NO light burning in the room. The najashi sat awake in a pool of moonlight, a cup of wine at his hand. Telemakos stood in the doorway.

"Young scorpion," Abreha said coldly. "What more is there to be said between us?"

"I want to buy Athena's passage back to Aksum."

Abreha looked down at his hands. He twisted his signet ring from his finger.

"And what can you possibly offer me in payment?"

Telemakos stepped lightly and swiftly across the room. His footfalls made no sound. He knelt before the najashi and pressed his forehead against the floor. The chimes at his elbow were silent. He moved with the sure stealth of a leopard stalking its prey.

"My service," Telemakos whispered. "I offer you my service."

There was a faint click as Abreha dropped his ring against the marquetry of his writing table. Telemakos waited.

Abreha picked up a taper and reached over with it to flick through the bells of Telemakos's bracelet. They rang and rattled.

"How do you do it? How do you move so silently?"

"I don't know. I am a good tracker. I have always been quiet."

Abreha lit the taper.

"As it happens," he said slowly, "I have need of your service, and you may not guess how it gladdens me that you offer it freely."

There was a small burner on the floor beside him. Abreha set about lighting it, and blew out the taper.

"All right, Morningstar. Get off your face. Come to your knees and listen to my proposal."

Telemakos rose, obediently, and sat back on his heels with his head bowed. The charms glittered, winking gold as the light caught them, but they made no sound.

"I want you to map the Hanish Islands for me."

Abreha placed a warming pan for mixing ink above the lighted burner.

"The skirmish in Adulis has not affected the negotiation over al-Kabir," Abreha said. "I am to meet with a representative of my cousin's there, to complete our transaction. I will travel in the flagship of my armada, as I did during Aksum's plague quarantine, with an escort of small warships to ensure my own safety in Aksum's waters.

"I'll put you aboard one of the warships, and you and they will leave the rest and navigate the archipelago in secret. I want you to sail the waters and walk the perimeter of the islands yourself, out of sight of the exiles and without the knowledge of my cousin's ships and servants, and draw me a true map of Gebre Meskal's prison fortress and its attendant islets. I want you to list any cove where a boat may find harbor, small or large, and any cave or inlet where an ambush may be placed on the island itself."

He paused. Telemakos was silent, thinking, I could do it. He knows what I did in Afar, now, and he knows I could do this, too. How long would it take—a month, two months? The najashi could kill me tomorrow, if I refuse.

"Is it true that Gebre Meskal means to forgive you for ignoring his quarantine?" Telemakos asked.

"I am building a church in his father's name, in thanksgiving that he has done so."

Gebre Meskal has got ships coming and going from Hanish, Telemakos thought, guarding the prison and negotiating with Abreha. Aksumite ships, bound for Aksum. Maybe when I have finished the mapping . . .

"I'll do it," Telemakos said. "If you swear by your dead children that you will send Athena home to our parents."

Abreha picked up his ring and dropped it in the warming pan. "By God, you young fox, I don't know where your loyalty lies, but you do not disappoint me."

"I can't decide which is the greater tyrant, you or Gebre

Meskal," Telemakos said. "In truth, aren't you and your cousin cut from the same cloth? He condemned an entire city to death in the name of his nation's good, and you spurned his sacrifice in the name of your own! My loyalty lies with Athena. I will not sacrifice my sister in my emperor's defense." He raised his head and added bitterly, "Nor any child."

Abreha rebuked him in quiet: "You are no longer a child, Lij Bitwoded Telemakos Eosphorus."

Now the najashi picked up a short penknife. He leaned forward and worked the blade's edge firmly beneath Telemakos's bracelet, and sawed through the thin silver strip. The chimes shook frantically for a moment, then the band fell away. Telemakos glanced down at the bracelet and spat on it. "Prove to me you'll keep your word and send my sister home. Swear by your dead children."

Abreha laid the knife down on his desk. He said gently, "Morningstar, I will not profane the souls of my dead children. But I'll give you surer proof than my word alone. I'll entrust you with my kingdom, if you dare to accept it."

In contemptuous disbelief, dumbfounded beyond fear, Telemakos raised his eyes to meet Abreha's, as one warrior might accept another's challenge. The najashi held his gaze.

"How are you going to do that?" Telemakos inquired as politely as he could, given that he was staring boldly into the najashi's face.

"By this seal." Abreha gestured to the signet ring that lay in the warming pan.

Telemakos began to guess at the najashi's intent. They were still eye to eye. He murmured, "Why doesn't it melt?"

"It is nickel, not precious metal. That little flame is not hot enough to melt it. It can be used as a brand, as well as a seal."

Then Telemakos lost all strength to speak. His question came out as no more than whisper, but still he stared brazenly into the najashi's face. "Do you brand all your servants?"

Abreha answered with quiet patience: "It is not the mark of a servant."

Telemakos remembered the touch of the smooth metal, after Abreha had sealed Telemakos's unsent letters with it, warm against the base of his skull.

"This seal on you will afford you protection within the bounds of my kingdom, and my own authority if you choose to wield it," Abreha explained. The najashi spoke seriously. He was not threatening; he was offering terms. "Accept the seal, and you accept the responsibility of carrying that authority as long as you remain alive, unless you tear it from your skin first. Misuse it, and you risk your sister's life. Or refuse it, with no honor lost, and trust me on my word alone."

Telemakos gazed into the najashi's sad black eyes beneath the heavy brow, and moved his lips to say, *I will accept.* But no sound came out. He licked his dry lips and managed to croak, less formally but with no less determination, "All right."

The najashi turned away first, graciously.

"Wait by the window, with your head on the sill. The mark

goes on the back of your neck, where it may be hidden by your hair. It is not meant to be disfiguring."

Telemakos moved to the window, thinking, I have spent a great deal of the past two years on my knees before Abreha.

He rested his cheek against the sill, feeling as if he were preparing himself to have his head struck off.

"You are fearless," said the najashi warmly.

"I'm afraid of dreams," Telemakos croaked.

"Yet you aren't afraid of pain, which is real, while the dreams are not."

Telemakos gave a hiss of sudden frustration, and found his voice again. "Must we discuss this like a pair of scholars? Do it!"

"The seal isn't ready," Abreha said quietly. "I can wait in silence, if you wish."

So they waited in silence, Telemakos with his head bent over the wide windowsill, watching the jeweled lights of the city above and below.

Abreha's narrow fingers smoothed back the hair at the base of Telemakos's skull.

"I doubt you'll ever thank me for this," Abreha said. "But perhaps you will forgive me."

Very gently, he kissed the back of Telemakos's neck to seal their contract, then pressed the mark of Solomon into his skin.

For one second the world was made of sparkling white light and blinding heat; then it was black. When he knew himself again, Telemakos was slouched against the wall below the window, sobbing childishly. The limewashed plaster beneath his cheek was damp with tears. He clenched his teeth and bit back the next sob.

He saw, rather than felt, that his hair was suddenly aflame. Abreha instantly beat it out with a damp cloth.

He *expected* this, Telemakos thought. He *expected* me to come to him. He *expected* he would be setting me this task, and sealing it like this. He had everything in place.

The najashi left Telemakos sitting by the window. He laid his ring in a dish to cool, and put away the tongs he had used to hold the heated metal. Then he slid his hand beneath the lip of his writing desk and sprang the hidden panel. He took a curl of palm tape out, closed the lid, and rolled the writing open on the marquetry.

"Your aunt has sent you a letter," Abreha said, "thanking you for the lion skin you sent her, and I see no reason you may not read it."

He *expected* me here, Telemakos thought again. He has saved this for last, to distract me, to court my favor, to reward my compliance . . .

But it worked. Telemakos crept to Abreha's side. The najashi held up the light in the burner so Telemakos might read.

Goewin's love and elation seemed to shout at him from the scratches on the narrow frond. Telemakos had the strangest sensation, shaping each word silently with his lips as he read,

that he knew exactly how each sentence should end, as though
he had read it all at least a dozen times before.

Telemakos my dear,

This gift, this prize
delights me! Never you the coward or
the fool, not with your father's strength and wit
and cunning bred in you to such degree.
A child no more, you've grown to manhood now.
Heed me, Telemakos.

He prowled among
the lions; he became a young lion,
and he learned to catch prey.

Few sons achieve
their father's stature. Most do not, and few
outstrip them. You, my soldier, you won't fail,
my bold hero. Beloved friend, you are
so well grown now, so wise, the flower of
the rising generation, and your deeds
will be their song.

Telemakos, heed me.

Your loving aunt, as ever, G.

The letter was in Ethiopic, but the inset quotation midway
through it was in Latin. This meant that the word *lion* was in

Latin, too; it would have been *anbessa*, Abreha's second name, in Ethiopic. So Goewin avoided making any connection between Telemakos's gift to her and the najashi's part in it. *How I love her*, Telemakos thought.

"May I read it again before you put it away?"

"Of course."

A child no more, you've grown to manhood now. Heed me, Telemakos . . .

He suddenly recognized the familiar rhythms of Homer's *Odyssey*. He reached out to touch the palm leaf, as if physical contact with Goewin's written words would bring him closer to his aunt, and at the second his fingertips brushed the inscription, he realized that the entire letter was composed of the goddess Athena's inspiring words to the prince Telemakos. The thrill of discovery and mystery that went through him felt as though it really did come straight through the scratched marks.

The phrases were out of context and out of order, but they were all direct quotations from his father's own Ethiopic translation of the first four books of the *Odyssey*.

Sphinxlike, Goewin had sent him a riddle.

Telemakos read it again. Only the lines in Latin were unfamiliar; they sounded biblical. Why had she used Latin? She could have written the whole thing in Ethiopic, or even in Greek. If it was from the Bible and the *Odyssey*, it was all originally Greek anyway. So why this verse in Latin? Why any of it?

He became a young lion.

Leo. Goewin had taught Telemakos the Latin word for lion on the day they met, nine years ago, when Telemakos had been no more than six years old. It was one of his earliest memories, how he and Goewin and Priamos, Gebre Meskal's ambassador to Britain, had exchanged names for his wooden Noah's Flood animals in three languages. Goewin had told him the British word for lion, also, *llew.* Her father used to call her twin brother, Lleu, the young lion. The Roman legate at Abreha's Great Assembly feast had called him that as well.

Leo. Llew. Lleu, who had once been prince of Britain, Goewin's twin brother. Medraut had also used the word *leo,* in the brief time he and Telemakos had been together earlier that year: *Spiderwebs joined together can catch a lion.*

Telemakos, heed me.

Telemakos's eyes were beginning to burn again. He could not unravel it. He had not enough time. It was not fair.

"Have you finished?" Abreha's even voice cut through his concentration.

"I've finished," Telemakos whispered. He watched the najashi's narrow, dark hands roll the palm strip shut.

"Muna, are you there?" the najashi called. The queen came in without answering aloud; only her clothes rustled and tinkled, as though, like a ghost, she had to make her presence known through the objects around her.

"Make a bed for the Morningstar in the sitting room," Abreha said. "Let him stay here tonight. You may want to anoint the burn."

Telemakos shivered. He reached up toward the blazing mark at the back of his neck, but thought better of it. Muna helped him to his feet, holding her resolute silence. Her touch on his bare skin was gentle and thrilling. Telemakos turned his flaming face away from her, ashamed of his tears and the turmoil in his stomach.

"Do you want an opiate?" Abreha asked him.

Telemakos bit back the bitter sarcasm that sprang to his lips: Why didn't you think of that before you set my hair on fire? He remembered his father, cold and courteous, held captive in chains that threatened to choke him.

"I'm all right," he said stiffly. He shrugged off Muna's simmering hands. "I told Athena she could have my dogs. She has promised to behave herself for you if she gets them. I left her sleeping in the Great Globe Room, and it would be a good thing if they were there for her when she wakes."

Muna beckoned him, one hand down, her fingers opening and closing by her side. Telemakos followed her out of the najashi's study and into the receiving room. She communicated without speaking, exactly as Medraut used to do, pressing Telemakos's shoulder to make him kneel and patting the shining ebony tabletop to make him lay his head down on it. She was sympathetic, but not shocked by the najashi's treatment of him; her manner was so firm and straightforward that he realized she must know more of Telemakos's misdeeds than he had thought. She was somehow Abreha's conspirator.

Her touch as she smeared aloe over the back of Telemakos's

neck was so delicate that he almost thought he was imagining it. But the brand itself felt like a small circle of flame at the base of his skull.

"Let me plait your hair," Muna said. "It will keep it off this wound, and you will look respectable for your interview tomorrow."

My *interview?* he thought, and suppressed a shudder, but the bells were gone and made no sound.

Abreha came through and stood watching as Muna began to comb Telemakos's hair. She scolded her husband sharply. "You might have waited to mark him until after your Federation lords interrogate him. Perhaps they'll find fault in him that you don't see."

"I know the worst already," Abreha answered. "He will withstand their questioning."

Telemakos dreamed he was in Afar, but the dream was unfamiliar. He lay on his stomach by a stagnant pool in a riverbed that was otherwise parched to dust. Above him, on the bank of the dry river, with the desert at his back, Goewin's slain twin brother, Lleu the Bright One, the young lion, the prince of Britain, whom Telemakos had never known in life, sat cross-legged. Lleu had Goewin's dark eyes and white skin, but in the dream he was the same age as Telemakos.

Telemakos lay with his left arm plunged to the shoulder in the still, green water, trying to tickle trout. But the pool was empty and the water was icy cold, and his arm had grown so numb Telemakos could not feel his fingers anymore.

He looked up at his uncle and said, "I can't do this. It will destroy me. It's not worth it."

"You must," Lleu answered. "You must show me how."

"There's nothing here," Telemakos said, and pulled his arm out of the water. But when he willed his black, frozen fingers to open, there on the palm of his dead hand lay Abreha's signet ring.

"That is the mark of Solomon," Lleu said. "You can keep it."

XII

A GUARD OF HONOR

THARAN WAS WITH Telemakos when he woke, pouring coffee spiced with ginger that Muna had left for them.

"The najashi has departed San'a. He is taking your sister to Aksum," the vizier told him. "Do not protest; we thought it best to spare you both a violent parting. When you've broken your fast, you may come with me to a gathering of the Federation so they may question you."

Telemakos could neither eat nor drink. Tharan sat patiently with him for a few minutes, then twisted the ends of his mustache and stood up.

"Let's go, then, boy. They will be waiting."

Tharan escorted him alone; no guard went with them. The stairways seemed eerily silent without the companion clash of tinsel at Telemakos's elbow. He thought again of Medraut and tried to carry himself with his father's fearless dignity.

"Lower your head," Tharan told him suddenly. "You must

not enter the Chamber of Solomon looking as though you have blood right to it. Your chances of withstanding this trial will be far greater if you do not seem prideful." He stopped, right there in the hall, and tipped Telemakos's head forward with a light touch. Telemakos stood still, seething, and fixed his gaze on his feet.

"Not so much," Tharan directed. "Show them humility, not shame. Are you ashamed of yourself?"

Telemakos did not think Tharan expected an answer to this, but he raised his chin, keeping his eyes cast down.

"Princely," Tharan said. "Perfect. Hold that. Can you?"

"Sir."

"I shall cough, to remind you, if I see you falter."

"I don't understand," Telemakos said quietly. "Why does it matter how I—"

He stood suddenly overwhelmed by his own perfidy, frozen, unable to step forward into this bleak, brief future he had created for himself, facing a lifetime's worth of fear and torment packed into a few weeks.

Tharan gripped him by the shoulders, as a soldier would his comrade before battle.

"Morningstar," he said, "do not be afraid."

Telemakos managed to swallow, and held his chin raised and his eyes lowered. He felt sure he must seem as demure as Muna as he walked into the assembly room where King Solomon was said to have held his councils.

Telemakos had no idea what to expect of this ordeal, but

his first shocked thought as he entered the arena was that he knew every one of his judges by name. There were sheiks he had met on his first day in Himyar, at the Governor's palace in al-Muza; others he had been introduced to and spoken with at the last Great Assembly of the Federation; Shadi and Jibril and Haytham of the Scions; and Malika's uncle Alim, who had traveled with them from Marib. Dawit Alta'ir the Star Master was there, representing his home island kingdom of Socotra.

And why isn't the najashi here himself? Telemakos wondered bitterly—but of course, the najashi was taking Athena to Aksum.

Telemakos stepped into the center of the room to meet the contempt of the gathered tribal lords. It had taken less courage to face down a pair of fighting lions.

His first interview lasted all that day. But it did not have the feel of the criminal trial Telemakos had expected. From the start it seemed far more like a scholar's examination than an inquisition. Dawit spent an hour quizzing Telemakos on his knowledge of Himyar's water: which provinces each wadi valley irrigated, how to harvest flood waters, the working of the wells beneath San'a, the depth behind the dams. It seemed unjust to Telemakos that he might be accused of treachery for possessing knowledge that his Himyarite masters had pounded into his head without his ever asking for it in the first place, but it also seemed pointless to pretend he did not know these things. So long as his questioners were focused on their own kingdom they did not touch on Aksum, and that was a relief.

The three Scions were given their fair turn to speak among the others. They sat together in a tense, conspiratorial knot. They avoided looking at Telemakos, but they were scribbling furiously back and forth among themselves on wax blocks the whole time, and Telemakos guessed they were probably more focused on him than anyone else there. They elected quiet Shadi as their spokesman. Shadi looked at him directly when he spoke, as a king to a supplicant. Telemakos kept his eyes lowered.

"Your loyalty is in doubt," Shadi said, a thing no one else had directly mentioned.

"My lord," Telemakos acknowledged.

"Jibril and I have good reason to uphold you, but Haytham wants you to account for your interest in Awsan."

"I have none," said Telemakos. "I've never set foot in Awsan."

Shadi directed his reply to the assembly as much as to Telemakos. He ducked his head and murmured in his half-embarrassed way, "Haytham observes, by your answers to the Star Master, that you're more intimate with Awsan's fruits and fields than he is."

"Anyone can memorize names and figures," Dawit snapped, "and it is a pity Haytham of Awsan has not applied himself better to the geography of his own kingdom. The Morningstar has never been to Britain, either, but he has got the measure of it in his head. Tell this assembly of Britain's principal rivers and where they flow, Morningstar, just as you have done for Himyar."

Half in disbelief, because it was so irrelevant, Telemakos spoke hesitantly. "Tamesis, in the southlands, flowing east; Sabrina in the west; and Tava in Caledonia, north of the Roman wall. These are the largest . . ."

Tharan coughed. Telemakos had raised his eyes, without thinking, to see if anyone was actually interested. He looked down quickly.

"Did you ever think to hear such a thing?" Dawit Alta'ir demanded of no one in particular, sitting back and picking leaves from his beard. "A young Aksumite speaking the names Tamesis, Sabrina, and Tava in Ghumdan's alabaster halls? He knows what he knows. Question him further if you are dissatisfied with him, my princes and my servants. Question him yourselves; I will not."

The interrogation lasted three days, not always under the same people. For its duration Telemakos was housed with the palace guard in their barracks. No one seemed specifically assigned to watch over him, but he was expected to adhere to the warriors' routine and standards and was never left alone. Each night before Telemakos slept, Tharan stopped by to bid him good night and to drip clean water over the burn at the back of his neck.

When the Federation assembly had finished with him, Telemakos started on the journey to al-Muza and the Hanish Islands to fulfill his pledge to the najashi. He traveled as one of a detail of young Himyarite soldiers. None of them towered over him as the cadets had done two years ago, though he was more slightly built than they; dressed like them for desert travel, and with his hair plaited tight against his skull, Telemakos looked like one of their number. Only he carried no weapon.

In the evenings, as they roasted partridge over a sage-scented cooking fire, the soldiers talked neutrally about hunting and the day's journey. Telemakos studied his companions' faces from beneath his lashes and wondered why these particular men had been chosen as his guard. Some of them were not very much older than he. He was curious about them but did not want to risk being cut cold by his only companions when they might be under orders not to speak to him casually. No one had said anything, in the middle of the first night out from San'a, when Telemakos had suddenly sat up sobbing aloud and calling for Kidane—*Save me, save me, Grandfather!* He would have been deeply embarrassed if anyone *had* said anything, so maybe they were just being polite. He did not want to have to explain the wound on his neck, either, and only rinsed it briefly when no one was looking.

He wondered how far ahead of him Abreha was, and if the najashi really did mean to take Athena all the way to Aksum himself. She is safe, isn't she? Telemakos fretted. I wouldn't finish the najashi's filthy maps for him if I didn't believe he would keep his promise to take her home. Is she safe? Why, oh why, would I ever trust her to *him*?

The burning sore at the back of his neck was all he had for surety. Each morning Telemakos woke with the feel of dried tears on his face. Half the time he could not remember what he had been dreaming of to make him cry. He wondered what his guards must think of him.

On the third evening of the journey, Telemakos tempted them to speak to him. He spread his complex instruments for measuring distance on a square of cloth beside the fire. It was like opening a box of magician's tricks: they had never seen a drafting compass or an astrolabe.

"How does that work? Is it a secret?"

"It's just a skill. Someone has to show you how the first time, and then you have to practice, just the way you learn to throw a spear. Pick it up and look, it's not magic."

"What do you use the wand for, if not magic?" One of them pointed hesitantly toward a straight-edge ruler.

Telemakos laughed. "That's for drawing lines! Are all soldiers so superstitious? Look, I'll show you . . ."

He showed them how to use the compass, too, and let the six of them each try it in turn, drawing circles in the bare ground where they had pulled up the grass around the cooking fire.

"With the star measurers you can reckon where you are, and how far you've still to go. I can figure the distance from here to al-Muza."

He could not do the calculations in his head but scratched figures with a finger in the dirt. His audience was so impressed by these occult tracements that Telemakos thought it would have disappointed them if he had announced a number directly without any show of conjuring it.

"Can you say what you are sent to do with these?" one of them, Harun, asked carefully.

Telemakos raised his eyebrows, as the Himyar children did in disapproval or denial, a habit he had picked up from Abreha's Royal Scions. "Of course I may not say," he answered.

Harun mirrored the gesture, understanding. "I should not have asked," he apologized. "I am always nosing to discover other people's errands." He laughed.

"Harun was brother-bonded to Asad, the najashi's eldest son, until he died," said Ghafur, whose handsome mustache was so fleetingly familiar that Telemakos always felt he was just on the verge of recognizing him as an old friend. "Do you understand what brother-bonding is?"

"Isn't it that your life is pledged as another child's servant, and the pair of you grow up together? As Rasha is to Queen Muna."

Ghafur blinked agreement. "Harun could never have waited on anyone else, only Asad; so after Asad died, Harun here was honored with a warrior's training. But Asad used to tell him everything. Harun knew all of Ghumdan's palace secrets."

"Oh. Not like me, then."

They looked so blank that Telemakos realized, with sudden surety and wonder, that none of his guard had any notion of his disgrace. He could not fathom what they must think of him.

"Were you all trained together?" he asked quickly.

"Not I," said Ghafur. "I'm newly sent from the garrison at Marib, for this detail especially. You know my father, Tharan."

"Of course, Tharan!" Telemakos exclaimed as he placed the naggingly familiar mustache. "You favor him exactly."

Then Telemakos was inspired. He took a dare on himself. He raised his head and tried to look Harun directly in the eyes, and then did the same to Ghafur, and all the other young soldiers in turn, finishing with Fariq, their captain. Each one deferentially looked away when Telemakos stared at him. So he knew they considered him their superior in rank, because he was surely not their elder.

"I like to nose in other people's business, too," Telemakos said. "You must tell me all your histories. I didn't realize you were so select a band. So you, Mahir, why were you chosen for this detail?"

"I am no one special. I am no prince's favorite servant or vizier's son."

Abreha's warriors always spoke like that. Telemakos thought their modesty must be part of their training. But the others laughed. Telemakos gave a little inward sigh of wonder and envy; they laughed so freely.

Their captain answered on Mahir's behalf. "Tharan says Mahir is the finest spearman he's ever taught. But I am their captain because, of us all, I am the only one who has seen combat. I was the najashi's squire at the battle of al-Muza."

All six of them had some royal connection or high rank or unusual skill. They were a privileged and intelligent elite among Abreha's young soldiers.

"I meant to flatter you when I called you a select band,"

Telemakos confessed. "I meant flattery, but you really are se-lect."

"Well, we know your full title," Fariq acknowledged, "though we've been told not to use it."

They thought his high rank was excuse for their own. That explained their courtesy. Still, why these six? Telemakos won-dered. Why these proud six to escort me, when brute strength would serve just as easily? The najashi doesn't have any reason to honor my ridiculous title.

On the fourth day they left the highlands and began their descent down the staired ways through the wadi valleys that drew off the mountain rainwater. Telemakos could make out nothing of the Hot Lands ahead, the low-lying plain of acacia and whining insects that lay between the mountains and the coast; the horizon was all steel-blue cloud. Late in the after-noon when, hours before sunset, the round red sun collapsed into this pall like a hot coal into ash, he realized it was not cloud, but smoke.

Wildfire crept across the lowlands and up the wadi valleys. It had been a dry year, and though the complex irrigation sys-tems of canal and well and reservoir kept the cultivated terraces green, wayside field and forest were brittle as tinder. At first the fire was all below them as they made their way cautiously down the main wadi. Then they found that there was fire smoldering in the dry brush at the edges of the staired ways. They could smell the smoke now, all the time.

They camped apprehensively. Unless there was a strong

wind in any direction, the fire was completely unpredictable. It crept in flickering zigzags through the undergrowth as though it were following some mysterious map of its own. They saw a running wall of knee-high flame leap an irrigation ditch and engulf an arbor, and yet the fire never reached the next level of the terrace, only eight feet higher up the hillside. At night they took turns to sleep. Telemakos was never made to wake more than one watch in any night; they babied him, he thought. But, of course, it made no difference whether he was awake or not, since one of them always sat guard over him, wildfire or no wildfire.

Oh please, Telemakos prayed silently, let the najashi be already safely past this with Athena.

The people of the towns and villages Telemakos passed through were all tense and tired. He and his guards had only a day's march yet to the Hot Lands when they came upon a group of farmers and officials arguing loudly, while onlookers raised their fists and hissed. Telemakos swerved from the main track toward the conflict without being aware he was doing it. Harun strode up beside him, herding him back to the road.

"Nosing in others' business?" Harun jested.

But the others were hesitating, too; the valley below them roiled with smoke. "Let him nose," said the captain. "It will give this inferno a chance to burn off."

They went in single file across a narrow ridge between two gullies so they might join the gathering. When they came closer, they could see that the crowd stood in a circle of ground at the upper edge of a sizable reservoir, half full. It was cleverly built into the hillside, and its walls formed the sides of the terrace below, so covered with grapevines that you would not know the reservoir was there unless you were standing on its rim.

A delegation from the besieged township lower down the valley was asking if the water could be tapped to help them fight the fires below. Their headman argued with a local official, back and forth, both of them stiffly courteous and neither yielding.

Telemakos was a slave to curiosity. He slid through the gathering to get closer to the arguing men. He loved the ease with which he could move among these folk who did not know him, now that he was out of San'a; his hair and eyes were always strange, but his skin was no darker or paler here than anyone else's. In Aksum, in his home, he had had to make an effort to be inconspicuous; in Himyar he blended well enough that he did not have to hide behind people. Infiltrating this crowd was easy. Harun managed to stick by him as he wormed his way to the front, but they left the rest of their band behind.

Telemakos saw how defensively the local spokesman stood, with his back to the sluices and his expression fixed and fierce, and felt instantly, inexplicably sorry for him.

"But I do not know what to do," this village official was saying unhappily. "I do not have the authority to divert this water. And what if the fire comes here, and I have spent Wadi ar Ramadah's reservoir on Wadi Risyan, what do I do then?"

"It surely will come here if it's not put out," the headman

from the lower township retorted angrily. "Do it to save your own crops if you must, your own homes if not ours; but do it now."

Telemakos listened to their exchange with interest and caution, as anxious as anyone that the grass fires on the lower terraces be contained, as otherwise he was bound to walk straight through them. And he was tired, despite the attention of his guard, nerves worn thin with flame and fear and grief. He was not looking forward to fighting his way across the Hot Lands.

"I do not have the *authority*," the reservoir's representative repeated slowly and emphatically, as though he were speaking to a child in a foreign language. "Do you think I do not *want* to help you? I do not lack sympathy. I lack authority."

Telemakos hesitated briefly. He had an idea that would either turn him into a hero or a fool. But it did not matter if he made himself ridiculous, and it might help; so he stepped decisively between the arguing men and knelt at their feet with his head bowed. He splayed his fingers across the back of his neck, framing the new brand that burned there, oozing red. It was healing slowly; he rinsed it daily, but he still had not dared to touch it directly.

"Here's your authority," Telemakos said. "Do what you need; hold me responsible."

He thought he could almost feel the heat of their stares, blazing down at him like flames fanned by the dry wind.

"That is the najashi's seal," the local spokesman and the visiting headman explained to each other, speaking both at once, and then they both went abruptly quiet, embarrassed and polite.

"Is it authority enough?" Telemakos asked, his head bent, still kneeling to show off the blaze.

"Yes, yes," said the spokesman in hasty agreement. "Indeed, yes. I would not have hesitated if I had known—"

"I will give you a lock of my hair, too, as proof that I was here and spoke to you, in case anyone questions your decision in weeks to come." Telemakos raised his head, elated and somewhat choked with mirth as he considered the trail of havoc he could leave on his way through Abreha's kingdom, wielding his own scorched, living skin as a weapon of unchallenged power.

He stood up. He was not exactly inconspicuous anymore; he felt as if he had just thrown off a disguise.

He asked, "If you really are going to drain your reservoir, can I watch?"

Harun was quiet, very quiet that evening as they camped. They had not built a fire themselves since they had left the highlands, not daring the risk of it spreading. And, too, they had been gifted generously with fresh bread and yogurt, and a skin of local wine, from the township with the reservoir. It was no great challenge for Telemakos to dip bread in yogurt and put it in his mouth. But Harun waited on him industriously, all the while holding this polite and fearful silence.

"Harun, have I offended you?" Telemakos asked at last.

Harun would not look at him. By now Telemakos was used

to the way they all lowered their eyes when they spoke to him, but now Harun would not so much as turn his face in Telemakos's direction. He looked at the ground as he answered with neutral respect, "Oh—indeed not, sir."

"Well, then, what's the matter with you?"

Harun drew a deep breath. At last he said evenly, "You know—we have said we know as little about you as you know about us. And none of us, yourself especially, is at liberty to tell why he's sent on a certain errand, or where our errands will bring us. I have today seen a thing, the mark of Solomon on your skin, that . . . maybe raises you in my esteem, but also makes me wonder who you are. And what you are."

Harun took another breath, and no one interrupted him. He had all their attention.

"Asad bore that mark, in the same place you bear it. The najashi's own son. It was there as long as I knew him."

Telemakos stared at Harun through narrowed eyes, astonished. But Harun was still glaring fixedly at the ground by his own feet.

"Maybe the najashi put his seal on you so that I would wait on you as I waited on his son."

Telemakos could never form any clear image of Asad in his mind: biddable Asad, whom Goewin had mistaken for a servant. Now this faceless boy had a brand on the back of his neck.

"It was to seal a contract between us," Telemakos said quietly. "If the najashi had wanted to bind his son to his service, perhaps he used it on him as well. Asad was his cupbearer."

"The najashi bears that mark also," said Fariq, the captain, he who had been the najashi's squire in battle. "Twin to the seal on his signet, burned into his flesh. In the same place you wear it, at the base of his skull." He added hesitatingly, "Do you forgive me the impiety, sir, but may I look?"

Their sudden heightened courtesy alarmed him as much as the hidden truths they were revealing. "What do you mean, Fariq, *the najashi bears that mark?* Oh, God's teeth, don't turn away from me like that!" Telemakos bent his head. "Go on and look, it's getting dark. *What do you mean?*"

They looked quickly, each in turn. It reminded him of the way the street children in Aksum used to line up to ogle a certain beggar, who had boasted an extra pair of shriveled legs growing out of his stomach and would show them to you if you paid him enough.

"Now *tell me what it means*," Telemakos demanded, and ordered fiercely, "Look up! Meet my eyes!"

"The najashi didn't always have the signet ring he wears now." Fariq met Telemakos's gaze for one brief, apologetic second and quickly lowered his eyes again. "His father's ring came to him after his brother Hector was executed, during the Aksumite wars. Abreha the Lion Hunter used to use the mark on the back of his neck to bear witness to his authority; I've seen him do it, just as you did this afternoon. In the early days of his Federation here, when he was newly come from Aksum, men respected his father's authority in that mark as much as they did Solomon's. Ras Bitwoded Anbessa, his father was called, the beloved prince Anbessa, the lion of Wedem.

"You bear Anbessa's title as well as his mark," Fariq reminded Telemakos.

"It's an Aksumite title," Telemakos said. "It doesn't mean much here. But I don't know, truly, *I don't know* all that the mark means. It was given me in trust, but I did not really believe it would give me the power to empty reservoirs and put out fire."

Once they reached the Hot Lands, they went a day and a half without stopping to sleep, to take them through the worst of the wildfire. When at last they did stop, Telemakos slept for fifteen hours. His companions, hardier than he, watched and hunted without him. He was annoyed afterward, when he woke and realized how much time had passed.

"You should have kicked me," he told his guard crossly. "I'm not a baby."

They laughed. "You're not a soldier, either," Fariq said. "There's no reason you shouldn't rest if you need to. We made good time yesterday."

Finally they left the fires behind. Apprehension of a different kind filled him as they approached the sparkling white domes and towers of al-Muza, which he had not seen since he arrived in Himyar nearly three years ago. He did not want to leave this band he had been traveling with. Suddenly the trying journey of the past two weeks seemed secure and un-complicated: a flight from straightforward danger, no need to plan or think, and a devoted retinue who brought him food and guarded his sleep. Desolation filled him as they escorted him along al-Muza's glittering streets between houses glazed with gypsum plaster. His warrior companions had treated him with kindness and devotion he surely did not deserve, and he would never see them again.

He had not realized how indelibly the open square with the fountains and black granite thrones was fixed in his mind until he was in the middle of it. He stood perfectly still for a moment when he recognized the place, shocked by the vividness of his memory. There was the condemned man still hanging here in his mind, the smell of blood and basil, and of Athena's sandalwood-scented hair and sweaty skin so close to his face, and the bitter taste in his throat and the feel of the lukewarm water of the fountain on his skin afterward, and the dying man's curse hissed at him: *Let the najashi hang you up in my place next, you unholy creeping mongrel spy.*

Fariq, the captain of his guard, grasped him gently by the elbow to press him forward. Telemakos started, and cast him an unguarded, stricken glance over his shoulder. He shook his head, desperate to get rid of the picture in his mind.

"What's the matter?"

"This is the place where criminals are executed," Telemakos answered, and added softly, "It makes me sick to stand here."

Fariq blinked. And then he said, with quiet sympathy,

"Whatever it is you're sent to do, Morningstar, I don't envy you."

They came finally to the wide white coral beach where boats landed and unloaded, and delivered Telemakos directly to a neat, slim fighting ship whose teak hull was painted turquoise, striped here and there with curls of white. You could scarcely tell where the ship and sea met, they were so similar in color, but for the watching black eyes painted on either side of the prow. The ship was pulled up in the shallows while men used hawri canoes and donkeys to ferry out a fresh water supply; the beach was covered with boards and mats and teeming with sailors and workmen.

Telemakos waited with his guard until the captain of the warship came to meet them. There was some confusion over who was in charge of him now, and the ship's master dismissed Telemakos's companions with brisk efficiency. They saluted him respectfully and left him with no other show of sentiment. They were lost in the crowd before they were thirty paces away.

"Apprentice pilot, eh?" the captain said, looking Telemakos up and down. "Are the tools of your trade covered in gold leaf, that you come so closely escorted? You're to have a personal guard on my ship as well. Whether that's for our safety or your own I've not been told. He's not here yet." The man raised his eyebrows in disapproval. "My outbound crew hasn't arrived, and I don't expect to have to watch you. You can sit in the hold until the najashi's new guard comes for you."

"Sir," Telemakos acknowledged coldly, handing over his satchel of cartographer's tools. He might have waited with his escort if they had not been so swiftly turned away.

"Go with the water bearers."

The compartment they found to use as a prison was so small a space between the hull and the forward oarsmen's bench that Telemakos could not sit upright after they had shut him in. Nor was there room for him to stretch out flat. It was pitch dark and ferociously hot, and stank of fish oil and the rank straw that lined the floor. Curled against the wooden staves, Telemakos did not dare close his eyes for fear that some dreadful memory would overpower him.

But nothing happened. Telemakos waited. The captain had left him a waterskin; Telemakos found he could manage to drink from it if he lay flat on his back with the skin on his chest. There was room for him to lie down if he pulled his knees up nearly over his head.

He slept without dreaming and woke to a commotion of voices and footsteps hurrying against the wooden planks. The siding that had sealed him in came away, and Telemakos screwed his eyes shut against the sudden light. When he dared to open them again, he was looking upside-down into the captain's face and at another man, a young warrior whose shadowy bulk made the ship's master look like a dwarf. The big guard laid his hand on Telemakos's forehead and gently forced him to turn his head aside, so that the back of his neck behind his right ear was exposed.

"Look," said the guard in a deep, rich voice. "Do you know what that is?"

The captain peered at the brand. Telemakos waited still, his joints so strained by confinement that he could hardly bear to contemplate stretching them.

"That is the najashi's seal," the captain answered in a low voice. "God help me. If I'd known—"

"You know now," said the guard. "Get him out of here, and bring him something to make a decent meal before we sail. I'll see to it he brings no harm to any of your crew."

The guard lifted him out gently. Telemakos tried to sit up but found he could not straighten his legs, and that his neck was so stiff he could not lift his head. Panic seized him, and he struggled.

"Stay calm," the young soldier said quietly, working his hands over the cramped muscles of Telemakos's legs. "There— stretch—now the other."

The captain helped, silent and guilty. Telemakos rubbed at the back of his neck as the two men set the sluggish blood moving through his body again. The brand was no longer sore. For the first time since Abreha had marked him, Telemakos tried to trace the outline of the najashi's seal. He could make out the points of the star, but the lion's head within the border was too fine for him to feel.

He looked up at the guard. The young man was a giant. Telemakos did not recognize his face, but he made a shrewd guess as to his name.

"Iskinder!"

The other stared at him in surprise, and Telemakos laughed, feeling obscurely pleased with himself. It was the young man on whose behalf he had asked Abreha to grant a recommendation.

"Iskinder of the al-Muza city guard! You of all men are commanded to be my watchman on this journey?"

Iskinder answered slowly, "I know you." He blinked in affirmation. "So I do. We met in the leatherworkers' suq, two years ago, and you had just stepped off an Aksumite ship. You were there with your sister and a lion. You gave your blessing to a crucified spy." Iskinder drew a breath. "You swore you would rather—" He stopped.

"—take such punishment myself than have to deal it out," Telemakos finished for him, gritting his teeth. He pushed himself up on one knee, getting ready for the effort it would take to stand. "So I said."

"You were right. It's a hateful task."

Telemakos shivered involuntarily beneath Iskinder's steely hands. Iskinder suddenly let go of him and drew back by a pace's length, leaving Telemakos a clear space in which to get to his feet himself.

Telemakos stood stiffly. The captain gave him his satchel.

"You're to answer to me," said the captain. "Iskinder is your guardian, but he has no right of command over you. It's a good thing you understand each other."

XIII

POPPY

THE VOYAGE TO the disputed Hanish Archipelago was swift but rough, and Telemakos was so wretchedly seasick throughout the day it took to get there that he thought his impending execution would bring nothing but relief in comparison. But soon enough they reached the looming volcanic peaks. In the shadow of Hanish al-Kabir the captain told him, "There's no landing place for a ship other than at the prison, on the western side of the island. We'll approach from the north, so they don't see us, and your guard can take you ashore over the reef. We'll follow you down the coast. There's not much tide here."

A thin mist of dull green scrub covered the lower slopes of lava. Below that, the coral sands shone white as bone dust. Iskinder paddled Telemakos to shore in a narrow hawri canoe and left him on the beach with a day's water and a box of wax tablets. In the afternoon Iskinder picked him up three miles to the south. The next day Telemakos spent shipboard, while the captain took soundings and Telemakos plotted them, so that they were charting the water as well as the land. They slowly made their way around the island.

To Telemakos, Hanish al-Kabir meant prison and plague, thirst and breathless heat, exile and war. And it was true that the island was nearly as dry as the Salt Desert. But it was so *beautiful.* On shore, alone, Telemakos would come around the curve of an inlet and find himself faced with a cliffside of flaw-less black rock, as sheer and smooth as silk, shot with veins of green like a dark emerald. The rock pools were seething with life: fish more bright than jungle birds, fish like needles of iri-descent glass, fish disguised as underwater flowers. Flamingos and spoonbills stalked among the coral in clear pale green wa-ter. Dolphins leaped beyond the breakers, where the volcanic slopes dropped steeply beneath the sea.

The beauty of it went to his head. Alone on the beach, Telemakos felt he owned it. Hanish al-Kabir did not belong to Abreha, or Gebre Meskal; neither one of them had ever set foot on it. It belonged to him, now, for every second of his limited life span that he stood as an illegal intruder on the shore with his ankles in the purling combers; the empty kingdom of sea and sky and sloping rock did not belong to him by right of deed or title, but by right of his being there when no one else was, by right of his astonishment at its unacknowledged beauty, and by right of his being the first to capture it truthfully in a map.

Each evening Telemakos transferred his day's notes to parchment in diligent detail. He took over the space at the bottom of the stepladder to the rowers' benches, out of the wind but still in the reach of daylight. He usually had some room to himself here, because the oarsmen preferred to sit above, in the full light and air, when they were not on duty. Telemakos spread his equipment on the floor and over the benches, working frantically in the scant minutes before dark fell; this final hour of the day was the most demanding for him, when his most precise work had to be done at top speed. Telemakos held the parchment in place with knees and toes, trimmed and cleaned his brush with his teeth, and deciphered his notes in the wax with his fingertips when he could no longer see them plainly. When he delivered the finished work to the captain and sat down on the deck to eat supper with Iskinder, he always felt exhausted and triumphant, as though the race against darkness actually pitted him against a physical opponent. Iskinder laughed at his ink-stained mouth.

"You are supposed to be inconspicuous!"

Telemakos finished his circumnavigation of al-Kabir and moved on to Zuqar Island. Quietly skirting the traders' outpost there, Telemakos considered what might happen if he did not meet Iskinder at the next inlet. Would they search for me? he wondered. If they missed me, could I then marry a fishergirl and spend the rest of my days diving for pearls?

He narrowed his eyes and kept going. One-armed pearl diver: it was stupid even to think about it, and anyway, he was branded with the najashi's mark. He could not hide that. If a hunt was made for him, no one would dare to give him harbor against the najashi.

In something more than a month the project was finished. They sailed back to the prison harbor on al-Kabir and anchored anonymously off the beach alongside a half dozen other sleek turquoise warships from Himyar, opposite a squadron of larger, seagoing Aksumite vessels. Iskinder in his hawri canoe took Telemakos and the completed maps to Abreha's flagship, which waited among its fellows.

The najashi's ship was larger than the warship Telemakos had grown used to, with a fully covered lower level for its oarsmen. Abreha had his own cabin, scarcely bigger than a cupboard, fitted with a worktable that folded down over most of the floor; Telemakos had to stand at the najashi's shoulder, there being no room to kneel, as Abreha paged through his new maps. He checked them immediately, even before he allowed Telemakos to ask about Athena.

"Tell me about this harbor."

"You can't see it from the water. You have to row around that headland to get in."

"Sheltered and hidden? And deep enough for a ship?"

"If you steer clear of the reef."

The najashi turned pages in silence.

"Fresh water here?"

"A rain pool."

"Springs?"

"There are two springs on Zuqar. You must know that.

There's a deep pool up the mountain on al-Kabir just here—I plumbed it. But you can't get there overland, and you wouldn't get a ship near the coast there."

Abreha said seriously, "These maps are *remarkable*, Morningstar. You've paid your sister's ransom and more."

Telemakos hesitated, then dared to ask at last, "Where is she now?"

"I left her in the port at Adulis, with your father, in the governor's mansion, your great-uncle Abbas's house. Abbas had sent a message to your mother to meet them there, but she had not yet arrived when I left. Athena is content enough, and safe. You may trust that, Morningstar. But it will be easier for you if you do not press me to talk about her over and over." Abreha prowled through the pages of maps again, handling them carefully. He said, "I wish I had given you more time."

Three days went by, and still they did not leave the prison harbor. Abreha went ashore each morning; the oarsmen were idle. Telemakos was not allowed on deck by daylight. Iskinder hovered near him, usually with his back turned apologetically, alert and wary.

Abreha asked Telemakos to eat with him, each night when he came on board his ship. "Why are we still here?" Telemakos asked on the third evening. The waiting made him want to weep and scream. It had not been so bad while he had work to occupy him, but in idleness his mind was left with nothing to do but construct his own execution a thousand times over. "Why not return to Himyar now? What are we waiting for?"

"I have a negotiation to complete with Gebre Meskal's representative and the warden on al-Kabir," Abreha told him. "You remember I had asked for release of certain prisoners there."

Telemakos drew a sharp breath. He said evenly, "Anako called Lazarus, former governor of Deire."

"Nothing escapes your attention, Morningstar."

The injustice of it so overwhelmed Telemakos that for several seconds he did not think he could breathe, let alone speak or put food in his mouth.

"I owe it to him," Abreha said sadly. "Surely you understand that."

"If you're securing his release," Telemakos said, "does that mean he will be aboard this ship when it sails back to al-Muza?"

"And if he is? How is he anything to do with you anymore?" Abreha asked. Telemakos pressed his lips together; he could make no answer.

"How, boy? Can he hurt you? Instruct you? Beg a favor of you? Can he send you to prison? Condemn you to death?" Abreha paused, waiting for an answer, while Telemakos, in polite and silent hatred, stared fast at a splintered place in the deck between himself and the najashi.

"He cannot touch you, Morningstar," Abreha said. "I understand why you should detest him; I do not like him, either, but to *fear* him, when you are utterly beyond his government? You manage your fear of me with grace and strength. What effort wasted, that you should spend your life in fear of such a one as Anako!"

He picked a comb of fine bones from his smoked fish and tested their sharpness with his fingertips. He looked directly at Telemakos from beneath his forbidding eyebrows. The najashi said, "Your fantastic title makes you his superior. I will require him to treat you with consideration, or suffer for it."

"Thank you," Telemakos said stiffly.

"I'm going ashore again tomorrow," Abreha said. "Would you like to work in my cabin, and make me copies of certain of your maps? I am sorry to keep you confined below, but I do not want you to be seen."

"Thank you," Telemakos said again.

"There are fresh pages and ink in the chest below the table."

"*Thank you*," Telemakos said through his teeth, and bent to his own meal, determined not to be forced to acknowledge any more of these courteous, meaningless offers of small kindness.

He spent the next day at the folding desk in the najashi's cunningly constructed cupboard workplace. Iskinder sat just outside, with his back to the entrance. The cabin did not afford Telemakos more space than he was used to, but it made a change from the monotonous horror of waiting with nothing to do. He was reaching for a new ink block when he discovered, rolled carefully behind the chest of supplies that Abreha had allowed him to make use of, the harness in which Telemakos had carried his sister at his side for the last two years and more.

For a moment Telemakos was defeated, too unhappy and tired to think. He sat on the planking beneath the folding easel with the saddle in his lap. It had grown too small for Athena, Telemakos admitted to himself now; even his charm bracelet had had to be lengthened during the time he had worn it, but nothing had ever been done about the baby's saddle. She should have learned to walk before she outgrew it. Why had Abreha kept it? Maybe it broke his heart, also, to part with Athena. Or maybe the najashi simply had not needed the harness as Telemakos had, having two arms, and had left it on board when he took Athena ashore. Telemakos slipped his fingers into the pockets at the side; Athena's finger dolls and the bone rattle and the wooden giraffe were gone. She must have taken them with her. Good.

Telemakos shook out the saddle's familiar folds. The tanned hide was worn supple and smooth, nearly black in places. He buried his nose in it and caught, past the smell of leather, a trace of flour and spice, the faint baked scent of his sister's skin. It made his throat ache with misery and longing. He took another deep breath, but the trace was gone; it was overwhelmed by leather and something like burnt poppy.

Poppy?

Telemakos glanced over his shoulder. Iskinder sat, as always, with his back turned. Telemakos hooked the shoulder strap over his head, so familiar a movement that again it made his throat suddenly close up with loneliness for Athena. He swallowed the loneliness and opened the saddle's inner pocket. The dozen vials and packets of opium that he had disposed of during his stay in San'a were still there, untouched. So were the original portions his father had sent with him.

Have I got enough here to stupefy everyone on this ship? Telemakos wondered. He calculated roughly.

Maybe not enough to immobilize them, but enough to get their guard down. In the waterskins? Will they taste it? The waterskins and the wine jars; it's more effective in wine. Then later, if enough of them are asleep, I can slip overboard and turn myself in to the Aksumite prison warden. Surely my own people will grant me sanctuary.

Telemakos shoved the vials and twists of paper into his own satchel and quietly folded his sister's saddle in its place behind the chest. He went back to work, wild hope bubbling within him like a springing fountain. It would be easy to get to the supplies; Telemakos had been left by himself with them in the lower deck several times every day. No one paid any attention to him down there; Iskinder sat at the top of the step-ladder, in the sun, and spoke to Telemakos only if Telemakos addressed him first. Telemakos had spent hours alone, the day before, watching one of Gebre Meskal's ships pull close to the beach so that men could slosh through the water unloading supplies for the prison.

"I've finished here," he said to Iskinder. "May I wait the rest of the afternoon below?"

"Keep your head down," his guard said, and guided him to

the ladder. Iskinder stayed at the top, waiting above with the rest of the crew as usual. Telemakos sat at the foot of the steps.

"Tell me when you see the najashi on his way back, will you, Iskinder? And if he is alone? He is setting free an enemy of mine."

After some time Iskinder called down to him, "They're on their way, just coming down to the hawris on the beach. Go take a look through the starboard oar holes at the back. Is that your man?"

Iskinder was above, watching the najashi and his attendants climb into the canoe, and Telemakos was alone for five minutes with the crew's water supply and enough opium to stun several elephants.

He glanced through the oar hole. He could not see the hawri on its way.

His conscience hammered at him so mercilessly as he worked that all the sweet hope was suddenly made bitter with guilt. If Telemakos escaped, Iskinder would take the blame. He would be stripped of his advancement, maybe whipped, set to labor, imprisoned. It would be the same for any other guard who allowed my escape, Telemakos reasoned, and I would not suffer such pity for a stranger, would I? But I am sorry for Iskinder.

Maybe that's why Abreha chose him for this job. He guessed how it would pain me to sabotage the one I had recommended, and then I might hesitate and fail to take my chance when it came.

But I'll not hesitate.

He worked over the storage vessels in silent efficiency, with knees and nails and teeth.

"Morningstar?"

Telemakos stoppered the last waterskin shut, bracing the skin in place with one foot.

"Sorry. I was thirsty, and it takes me a long time to get one of these open."

"I'd help you. Anyone would help you."

"I'm all right."

Telemakos had drunk as much as he could hold, before he had started. He did not know when he would next find uncontaminated water.

He folded himself into a corner of the hold with his knees against his chin to wait, but the najashi found him there. Abreha came down the narrow stepway past Iskinder and beckoned Telemakos to his feet.

"Come up. You must share this ship with your enemy for a brief time, and I do not like to see you skulking down here as though in cowardice."

Abreha bent to one of the waterskins. He refilled his own leather bottle, drank from it, and offered it to Telemakos. Telemakos refused quietly.

"I'm all right."

"Come up with me." The najashi laid his hand across the back of Telemakos's shoulders to propel him in the right direction.

Anako the Lazarus sat cross-legged and hunchbacked on the deck, a withered, sunken bundle of rags and bones. He had been heavy before his exile; the flesh hung off him loosely now, and his gray hair was so thin it looked as though his bare scalp was brushed with dirty cobwebs. He had been an evil man, and for all Telemakos knew, he was still evil; but he was also old, and ill, and frail, and without any power.

He had not forgotten Telemakos. When Anako raised his head, his look was filled with hatred.

"This is Lij Bitwoded Telemakos Eosphorus, the Morning-star, who has just completed an apprenticeship with my car-tographer," Abreha said. "I am aware you know each other of old, and have reason to consider yourself opponents. But you have both done me faithful service, and while you are guests aboard my flagship, you must be civil toward each other, and dine together with me." Abreha turned to Telemakos and commanded, "Show this man a sign of your goodwill."

Telemakos held out his single hand to Anako, palm down, a gesture of sure and cold command. Anako hesitated, glancing up at Telemakos in disdain and disbelief. Telemakos turned his hand slightly, so that its slant presented the two scarred fingertips; that was where Anako had maimed him. There was another scar on his shoulder where Anako had tried to kill him.

Telemakos saw that the hateful, cringing man before him did not recognize the wounds or remember inflicting them. Anako looked blankly past the uneven fingernails, focused simply on the distasteful task of giving Telemakos some formal greeting of respect.

"I remember you," Anako hissed. "You sentenced me."

"Anako of Deire," the najashi said grimly, "was he not merciful in his sentence? Are you not alive, and free, and whole? Might he not have sent you to your death? The Morningstar has offered you his respect. Make your peace."

Anako took Telemakos's outstretched hand, and the second that he did so, before Anako could consider what he would do next, Telemakos bent quickly and laid a light kiss on the back of Anako's thin and brittle knuckles. He dropped Anako's hand and straightened his back. Abreha brushed the brand at the back of Telemakos's neck with light fingertips. The touch made him shiver.

"Superb, my Shining One," the najashi murmured approvingly. "Now let us eat together."

That night Telemakos waited quietly in the dark, sitting at Abreha's side and biting his knuckles, while as if by some enchantment all those around him fell quietly into drugged sleep. Abreha was among the first to go, Iskinder among the last. It was astonishing for Telemakos to watch it happening, knowing he was responsible.

Spiderwebs joined together can catch a lion, he thought.

"Your enemy is not very frightening," Iskinder remarked. Anako was a shambles of a man, sprawled asleep on the deck with his mouth gaping. The skin of his feet and hands was cracked and scabbed. "The state of him! I do not know whether he is in the greater part disgusting or pitiful."

"He's pitiful," Telemakos said quietly, amazed that for the past three years this wretched man had haunted his night-mares. "Hard labor and poor food wear your body down."

How I feared and hated him, Telemakos thought; Anako and his henchman Hara the Scorpion. And Hara ended up crucified as a spy, and here is Anako, a broken old man. In the end all my fear is gone. How can it have happened? But there's only pity left.

Telemakos sat quietly, waiting. After a little while he began to wonder if he had overdone the dosing of the wine and water. The drugs had been given to him for use as painkillers, not as sedatives. He had not really expected everyone to end up snor-ing on the deck around him. But even Iskinder fell at last.

If I've missed anyone, he will raise an alarm, Telemakos thought, and waited, and waited, until the half moon jumped suddenly out from behind the heights of the island, and washed the quiet sea with silver. Abreha slept peacefully, his troubled frown relaxed, one narrow hand laid over his chest and gently rising and falling as he breathed. The lion's head on his finger rose and fell with his hand, as though it were alive.

Telemakos saw that he could become an assassin, now, if he were bloody minded. But there was only one thing Telemakos wanted in this moment of advantage over Abreha, and that was the death warrant that he kept folded in his sash. Tele-makos lifted Abreha's hand from his chest and pulled back his robe. There at his waist was the familiar, detested parchment, smooth and supple with wear, the sealing wax recently renewed. The lock of Telemakos's own hair glittered like a shaving of salt in the moonlight.

Telemakos meant to destroy the warrant, but once he had taken hold of it, he could not resist reading it first. Everyone was so fast asleep. He rooted through Abreha's cabin to find a taper and steel and flint. He was as awkward as a baby with the fire-lighter, having to use the edge of his foot to hold it steady, but at last he made himself a light to read by. He bit through the seal on the document and opened the page with trembling fingers. The writing was in Latin, and although Telemakos spoke it flu-ently, its written alphabet was the least familiar of the handful of languages he could read. After he had struggled through the opening paragraph he stopped in puzzlement and began again.

> To the noble Abreha Anbessa, najashi etc., a copy of a declaration to the Aksumite emperor Gebre Meskal, from Constantine son of Cador, high king of Britain. Translated and transcribed by the hand of Priamos Anbessa of the Aksumite house of Lazen and Ambassador from Gebre Meskal to Constantine.

Whatever it was, it was not a warrant for his execution. It was a copy of a letter to Gebre Meskal from Constantine, Britain's high king. It had been dictated to Priamos, Britain's Aksumite ambassador at the time the letter was written, who, like Abreha, had been trained as a translator. Telemakos skipped down the page to read what Abreha had written at the bottom, in South Arabian, on that evening when he caught Telemakos ransacking his study:

I, Abreha Anbessa, mukarrib over the Federation of the Himyarite tribes and kingdoms, have read and understood. As of this writing Telemakos Meder is unaware of his British duty. Toward my benefit and the boy's own safety he shall not know while he remains my ward, nor shall any other man of my kingdom. In my care he shall not be addressed by his British title nor by his father's name. I may not destroy this document, my proof of what I hold, but this day I reseal it against prying eyes, and bind the child's secret with a lock of his own hair. Any who finds this sign and my double seal broken, or who has not my word, reads this without authority.

Telemakos gnawed at his lower lip, frowning.

What is this? Abreha said it was a death warrant, didn't he? What did he say—

In the hands of your enemy this is warrant for your execution. But let us keep it safe in the hands of your friend.

So *what is it?*

Telemakos held still and listened. All was silent on board; the sea lapped against the hull of the ship, the floats and buoys rattled, and somewhere on shore came the ringing of a lone hammer from the obsidian works. That was all the sound there was. Telemakos bent quivering over the hated, mysterious parchment and read Constantine's message to Gebre Meskal and Abreha:

The high king sends these words:

"This evil plague has cost me more than life itself, for I have lost my queen and two small children. I must marry again, but I am sick at heart in doing so, and fearful of my own mortality. Until I may declare otherwise, I name as my heir Telemakos Meder, grandson to my lord and late king, Artos the Dragon. The child has been raised an Aksumite citizen, but his father, Medraut son of Artos whom you name Ras Meder, will attest to his British royalty.

"Goewin, Artos's own daughter, has long sworn to Lij Telemakos's suitability for this position, and once proposed to make him Artos's heir herself. So I name him prince of Britain, to become high king after my death, and beg your protection of him until such time as he may be needed to fulfill his duty in the land of his fathers."

Telemakos stared blankly at the page, trying to comprehend what he had just read.

I name him prince of Britain, to become high king after my death.

He read it again, carefully, and then again, with Abreha's postscript.

Toward my benefit and the boy's own safety he shall not know while he remains my ward, nor shall any other man of my kingdom.

"Prince of Britain," Telemakos whispered aloud.

This is what Goewin was trying to tell me. *He became a young lion.* And I nearly guessed it, too; I dreamed of Lleu the night after I read her letter.

Telemakos laid down the page and touched the branding at the back of his neck.

He thought: Abreha has known this since the day I found the map of Hanish in his office. No, before that. He has known it as long as I have lived with him. This is why he kept my letters from me. This is why he would not let my father talk to me. *This* is why he has no British ambassador; anyone from Britain would have told me.

A cold wave of understanding took him with all the violence of a winter's monsoon.

Abreha has been holding me hostage for two years.

Oh, the serpent, the *serpent*, how he has deceived me!

The moon had traveled more than ten degrees up the sky since Telemakos had found the letter. He looked up, and felt a stab of panic at the time he had wasted.

Should I take this with me, he wondered, looking at the page. The parchment rippled silver in the moonlight, the blocky Roman letters as black against it as the lava slopes of al-Kabir. *There is nothing you can take from me which I would not forgive you,* Abreha had told him. *Except knowledge.*

No, I can't, Telemakos decided. It would probably be ruined in the sea if I took it. I suppose it doesn't matter; I meant to destroy it anyway—but now that I know what it is, I don't really want Abreha to know I've seen it. I'll leave it with him. But I'll have to—

The desire to pay back deception for deception was irresistible. Telemakos nearly laughed aloud, wild with mirth.

I'll have to reseal it.

He gently coaxed the ring from Abreha's hand and set to work at the najashi's desk. He had to hold a strand of hair fast in the corner of his mouth while he hacked it off with Abreha's knife, and he burned himself with the sealing wax in his nervousness. It was a murderous fiddle teasing the lock of hair through the slits in the parchment, but he managed it at last. Telemakos slid the ring over his index finger so he would not lose it in the dark, crept back to the sleeping king, and folded the sealed letter back inside Abreha's sash. The heavy signet caught the light of the moon and winked like a fish scale against Telemakos's ink-stained fingers.

Deception for deception, Telemakos thought. I'm going to keep his seal. Like Menelik did with the Ark of the Covenant, when he fled from Solomon. I wonder what Abreha expects as my ransom.

He tucked Abreha's ring in his cheek. It was too big for him to wear comfortably, and he did not want to risk losing it in the water. He took off his shirt and sandals, and dressed in nothing but his kilt, slid down one of the tie lines into the harbor.

He could not lower himself by degrees, and fought against his weight in his effort to avoid the noise of a splash. Wherever his skin met the rope it was stripped like meat. Telemakos gasped as the burning salt water closed over the raw flesh, and clung close to the mooring for a minute, adjusting his body to this strange new world of water and darkness. He kept his lips pressed together fiercely, sipping air through the corner of his mouth. He was determined not to lose Abreha's signet.

There. So, next. I go on.

The children of the Aksumite highlands were not swimmers, but Medraut had seen to it that Telemakos could manage himself in deep water. It did not frighten him, and he knew he had not far to go. He made his way from line to line and at last to the shallow water of the coral beach. A prison guard waited for him there, carrying a dark lantern and a long knife.

Telemakos wiped his nose and coughed, and the ring was cupped in his fingers. He knelt, and the ring was hooked over one of his narrow toes with the intaglio curled tightly under the ball of his foot, covered in sand. Telemakos raised his head and said loftily, in his most formal, palace-polished Ethiopic, "Deliver me to the warden."

The patrolman said quietly, "Just who the devil are you?"

Telemakos resisted the wild temptation to introduce him-self as prince of Britain. His Aksumite title was a deal more probable.

"I am heir to Aksum's imperial house of Nebir," Telema-kos said, with no less arrogance, but with such sure authority that the man held quiet and let him speak. "I have been made hostage by the Himyarites, and I beg you to deliver me to the sanctuary of my own people."

The sentry gazed down at the dripping, half-naked boy who knelt before him, and said, "Minor Aksumite prince, or run-away oarsman? How am I to tell?"

"You must surely know that none of these fighting ships are manned by chattels," Telemakos answered evenly, "and should you shine your lamp direct upon me, you will assure yourself why none would want my service as his oarsman in any case."

The guard sheathed his knife and slid open the shutter of his lantern so that the light fell full in Telemakos's face. Tele-makos blinked and winced away; the light followed his glance, and spilled over his bare and glistening shoulders. There was a moment of stillness.

The man cleared his throat and shuttered the lamp again. "I see. Come, then."

The sentry drove Telemakos before him, shivering, as they sought out several other guards and told them where they were going, and warned them also to focus their attention on the beach where Telemakos had turned up, should the self-styled heir to the house of Nebir be hunted or prove to be lying, and then, with increasing hope mingled with the fear that he would never really get away from the najashi, free, still with Abreha's signet ring now clutched undiscovered in his flaming palm, Telemakos came into the gatehouse of the emperor's prison.

XIV

A HANDFUL OF OBSIDIAN AND PEARLS

THEY HELD HIM, guarded, in a windowless room of black stone like a cave. They had a brief argument over whether to wake the governor of the island and decided that they would. No one had ever turned up on the doorstep of the prison on Hanish al-Kabir and begged to be let inside. Telemakos stood quietly picking his hair out of Muna's plaits with thumb and forefinger, as much out of a sudden urgent need to put Himyar behind him as to hide the ring in his palm.

After a short time the governor came in, hastily dressed but wide awake. He was a short, broad-shouldered man with gray hair, and he had the unmistakable hard authority of an old soldier, probably a veteran of the last conflict between Aksum and Himyar. Telemakos bowed and knelt, waiting for permission to speak.

The man drew a deep and shuddering sigh before he said anything.

"Lij Bitwoded Telemakos Eosphorus."

Telemakos glanced up, startled.

"How do you know me?"

"How should I not know you? Have I not sat all this week in negotiation with a collection of nobles from three empires, arguing over your fate?"

Telemakos narrowed his eyes, random scraps of knowledge locking into place like fragments of a puzzle. All the commotion over Anako's release had been part of Abreha's design, a smokescreen to keep Telemakos unaware that he himself was the real object of everyone's attention.

"Lij Telemakos, you look cold," the warden said. He unwrapped his own shamma shawl and threw it over Telemakos's maimed shoulder. He raised Telemakos to his feet. "Please, your highness, do not kneel to me."

The sentries bowed their heads, and Telemakos's heart swooped nearly into his throat at being addressed so formally. *Prince of Britain.* He tucked the ends of the shamma in place, embarrassed at his sudden elevation from runaway bondservant to the dramatic focus of conflicting nations. "God reward you, sir," he said quietly.

"Get me a hawri," the warden told the sentries. "We'll take him across to the general."

Telemakos was escorted, now, rather than driven. They took him back to the water's edge and helped him into a canoe. His deliverers carried no light and crossed quietly to the Aksumite ships. In the dark, men whispering hoarsely to one another in Ethiopic fixed him in a rope sling and lifted him on board.

In the lantern light on this new deck Telemakos saw the face of the man who met him there: a familiar, heavy, disapproving brow and high, narrow cheekbones. There was no ring decorating the dark, fine hands that held the ends of the rope that was fixed around Telemakos's waist; the ring that should rest there was on Telemakos's finger now, clutched tight in his palm, damning him. Telemakos gave a wordless cry of despair, sure that Abreha had second-guessed him yet again. He tried to throw himself backward into the sea.

"Telemakos!" The voice he knew so well rapped out his name in a soft, sharp, commanding bark. "Telemakos, I am not Abreha!"

Telemakos turned his head. He had lived with Abreha so long that it had slipped his mind how similar the najashi was to his own younger brother.

"Ras Priamos?" Telemakos guessed.

"Peace to you, Telemakos Meder," said Priamos Anbessa. "You've been lost."

On hearing his own name Telemakos was so awash with relief that he stumbled, and found himself sitting on the deck. By force of habit he climbed to his knees and tried to make a formal bow, but Priamos gently pushed him back down.

"Sit. Rest. Why have you been released? Are you a messenger?" Priamos quickly untied the supporting rope. "Abreha had not yet agreed to our contract!"

"I ran away." Telemakos let the corner of his mouth quirk into its crooked smile. "I put the najashi and his men all to sleep with opium, and left them."

Priamos laughed. His delight broke up the angry look of his heavy brow, just as it did Abreha's. "Ah, heroic!" He was still laughing as he looked Telemakos over in the moonlight. "Never in my life have I had the upper hand over my brother! You're not hurt, are you?"

"Just wet. The prison warden gave me his shamma, but my kilt is soaking through it."

"Have mine. Take off your kilt so it can dry out. You'll have to do without shoes till we reach Adulis, I fear." He took Telemakos by the wrist to help him unwrap his shamma; the heavy nickel ring blinked silver against Telemakos's dark knuckles.

Priamos stared in stunned silence. At last he breathed a long, shaking sigh. When he brought himself to speak, it was in a whisper. "That is my father's crest. That ring belonged to my father, Ras Anbessa, the Lion of Wedem."

"So it did," Telemakos answered in a low voice. He had not thought of that, when he took it.

"I last saw it on the hand of my elder brother, Hector, before he went to battle against Abreha in the past conflict with Himyar," Priamos said quietly. "A dozen years ago now. Abreha's men must have delivered it to him when Hector was killed. How have you come by it?"

"I took it from the najashi, just now, as he slept. I took it because—I don't know why I took it. Petty vengeance, I suppose.

He had—he used it to brand me. He burned the mark into the skin at the back of my neck."

Priamos reached out a hand to tilt Telemakos's head aside, moving so suddenly that Telemakos nearly lost the ring.

"Shine a lantern here, someone!"

Telemakos bent his head beneath the light while Priamos pushed back the wild hair.

"Mother of God. I did not believe him—Not you, boy, I did not believe Abreha. He says he does not want to release you because he has made you his heir. How should any of us believe such a fantastic tale, when all we know is that he has held you imprisoned and helpless in a tower of Solomon's palace for two years?"

Telemakos shook his head, understanding none of this.

"Telemakos Meder, if Abreha has put this mark on you, it means he counts you as his own son."

Telemakos jerked his head from Priamos's grip and said sharply, "Do not *mock me!*"

"I don't. Look."

Priamos bent his own head to the light.

"Look well," he said, and pulled his shirt away from his neck. His hair was cropped close to his skull, and the lines of the scar shone clean against his dark skin, the familiar lion's head within the five-rayed star.

"But—" Still it meant nothing to Telemakos. "But you aren't Abreha's son!"

"I am Priamos Anbessa," Priamos said quietly. "I am called

lion, Anbessa, after my father, as is Abreha Anbessa. I am marked with the lion seal of Solomon as are all Ras Anbessa's sons. The man who branded you bears the mark himself."

"So he does." Telemakos blinked, then nodded, falling back into Aksumite ways. "I know. But I thought . . ." He felt suddenly idiotic that he had not realized his full worth to Abreha. "The najashi isn't allowed to appoint an heir without his council's approval, and they have not tested me . . . Oh, but they *have*! That was my *interrogation* . . . And he led me to believe I was on trial for treachery!"

Telemakos stared out over the dark harbor, sending winged thoughts toward Abreha's ship.

I did not need such proving, my najashi. I might have been more faithful if you had been kinder.

He was suddenly overcome with exhaustion.

"Can I sleep here?" he asked.

Priamos and his companions unearthed a grass mattress and an elegant, light blanket that felt like a weave of silk and wool; they left Telemakos alone with a jug of water and a jug of wine, and cold fried bread and dried dates folded in a square of linen.

He was not hungry, and once he was dry he did not need the blanket. But Telemakos could not go to sleep. He lay staring up at the sky's familiar map of stars passing slowly and inevitably along their appointed paths. His cool, perceptive tracker's mind began to make sense of all that Abreha had done over the last two years, and as with Anako, the overwhelming emotion that took hold of him now was not anger, or hatred, but pity.

I betrayed him *before* he marked me as his son. He knew, and marked me anyway.

That means he has already forgiven me.

Telemakos opened his eyes to fast-moving clouds scudding high overhead in a blue sky. He sat up.

"Ah, you have outdone your grandmother the queen of the Orcades this time, scheming young witch's spawn," Goewin said merrily, flying to his embrace. "I doubt if even Morgause ever knocked flat twenty-eight men with one blow. Half of them are still asleep, including our najashi, so he has not yet learned of your perfidious nature—well, perhaps he already knows."

Goewin held Telemakos off, so she could look at him. "Heavens, don't weep, boy."

"I'm not. It's the light." Telemakos swiped at his eyes, and asked hopefully, "Is my father here, too?"

"This is not his negotiation." Goewin was cool. "He has no business representing Britain here; that is my role in the Red Sea. Medraut is . . . he has no match as warrior and hunter, but he is too headstrong for true diplomacy. I have made him wait for you in Adulis, with your mother and your sister."

"Ah, Goewin, truly? Athena, safe, with my mother and father?" Telemakos could not help himself. He burst into tears.

Goewin waited. Then she smiled at Telemakos, doing small motherly things like tucking his hair back from his face and pulling his borrowed shamma straight. She wiped his eyes with the shamma's edge. "Shame on Ras Priamos," she said, "taking all the credit for your deliverance last night, and not telling either one of us the other was aboard! He didn't want to wake me—"

Telemakos saw that his aunt's smooth, white face had become faintly lined, like his father's but not so deeply, and that her eyes were red rimmed and blue ringed, as though she had not passed a full night's sleep for weeks and weeks.

"—I negotiated like this with your father, over Lleu's life, years ago," she said. "It was a simpler battle then, good and evil clear to me, Medraut wrong and contrite, no ransom paid. God grant this is the *last time* I have to win freedom for the prince of Britain! If it happens again, you're on your own, boy."

"What's my ransom?" Telemakos asked.

"These damned islands, of course."

Telemakos was speechless. He gazed upward toward the black volcanic heights; the noise of the quarry was loud and busy now, and a patrol of pelicans skimmed the horizon between sea and sky.

"Are they worth so much?" he asked finally, rather awed. Goewin burst into laughter.

"Are *you* worth so much, you mean. Pestilent son of a demon, Gebre Meskal has entailed these lumps of rock to you to buy your freedom with."

"What do you mean?"

Goewin held up a small linen bag, richly embroidered. She untied the silken cord that shut it.

"This," she said, "is your symbolic right to the land here. Hold forth your hand."

She poured into his open palm a handful of obsidian chips and slivers of polished tortoiseshell, coral beads, and pearls.

"This is yours, just now: the Hanish Islands and the wealth they offer. In truth, the islands are a gift to you. Gebre Meskal has long owed you a debt of gratitude for your service in Afar, and the warning that you sent him through your father has made him eager to repay you. The archipelago is yours by the emperor's decree, and became yours in deed when you set foot on Hanish al-Kabir—Why, what is so gaspingly funny about it?"

Telemakos was choking with laughter. "I knew it!" he spluttered, coral and obsidian falling over his knees as the beads slipped between his fingers. "I knew it—I stood on the shore and in my heart I owned it! I stood kicking up seawater on the reef north of the prison and imagined myself king of the starfish! I knew—"

He gasped and swallowed. He had not eaten for nearly a day, and he was intoxicated with the audacity of his escape. "Anyone might do the same," he said, more soberly but still breathless. "Anyone could stand there and feel that way. It is so *beautiful*. If I give it away this afternoon I will still feel like I own it. It means *nothing* who owns it in deed."

Goewin gathered the spilled tokens of Hanish's wealth into a pile. She laughed as well. "It means a little, Telemakos. It means you may buy your own freedom. It is only a formality, of course, but I thought you would like to take hold of your fate yourself when the contract with Abreha is finally sealed.

"Or," she added slyly, "you could keep the islands, seeing as you have jumped ahead of your najashi's plans and struck out for freedom on your own."

"You can see Hanish from al-Muza," Telemakos said. He held forth the rest of the handful of jewels for her to put back in the bag. "You can see the peaks. It only takes a day to reach the islands, if you sail from Himyar. Of course they should belong to the najashi. What should I gain by keeping them—a new war between Aksum and Himyar, *on my account* this time? God forbid me!"

"You have grown, Telemakos," Goewin said softly. She tied shut the little bag that contained his freedom, and sat back on her heels to gaze at him. "Mercy on us, I think you must be as tall as I am. Stand up and let me see."

They climbed to their feet together. He was the taller by a fraction. Impulsively, she gave the back of his single hand a quick, reverent kiss. "'Beloved friend, you are so well grown now, so wise—'" She quoted the goddess Athena briefly, and laughed again, her faintly lined face made young and bright with joy. "Dear one, you cannot know what a weight has lifted from my heart this morning."

It was late in the day before a party came paddling over to them from Abreha's ship. The najashi's hawri pulled alongside them and Abreha rose up on his knees, brandishing a scroll of parchment. Goewin, with Priamos firm and frowning by her side, leaned over the rail to shout at him. Her high spirits had not waned all through the hours of waiting for this moment.

"Well met again, Abreha Anbessa, Lion King of Himyar!"

Goewin beckoned Telemakos forward and gripped him by the shoulders, so that she and Priamos flanked him protectively, like the emperor's spearbearers. But when Telemakos leaned over the rail, Abreha did not speak. He gazed up at Telemakos in silence.

Telemakos did not look away. Long seconds passed, and after a time the sounds of wind and sea and the noise of work in the prison quarry seemed to become oppressively loud.

"My najashi!" Telemakos called down. "Please don't punish Iskinder."

Abreha only glared up at him accusatorily, until Telemakos felt almost desperate that the najashi speak to him.

"I'm sorry I poisoned your crew," Telemakos offered. He was in truth rather appalled at the number of men he had laid low in making his escape. He was not sorry for any of the rest of it.

Abreha stated coolly, "You swore to me once that you are not a thief."

"I am not a thief," Telemakos retorted. "I am about to pay off all my debt to you. And anyway, you swore to me that you would forgive me anything but knowledge."

"I did *what?*"

"On the night you sealed our covenant. Our first covenant,

when you told me you had written out my death warrant. You held the mark of Solomon before me on your open hand, and said, 'There is no tangible thing you could take from me that I would not forgive you.'"

The najashi knelt upright in the bobbing hawri, frowning thoughtfully. Then light seemed to break across his face, and he was smiling his joyful, child's smile. "I remember. And you, silver-tongued sycophant, compared me to Solomon in my wisdom and forgiveness."

Abreha threw back his head and laughed.

"I suppose I must forgive you, then, if I already gave my oath that I would."

"My najashi," Telemakos called, and managed to keep his voice from cracking. "Mukarrib, Federator of Himyar! I would like to link the Hanish Archipelago with your Federation!"

"So be it!" Abreha cried. "So be it. By heaven, you shall seal this contract yourself. You may keep my ring, on condition that you wear it, King of the Pearl Fishers! You may keep it, on condition that you bring it back to Himyar on your one fine hand, as my son should have done, if it is required of you! I will forgive the mark you took from me, if you forgive the one I made on you!"

Telemakos lightly touched the seal at the back of his neck, and thought about the pact he was about to enter into. The threat of death was gone, but it had never been real. The danger of death was real, and would be there always. All the old bonds were still in place and more: his service to the najashi, and the emperor, and the high king.

"You should have been plain with me," Telemakos said. "You should have told me what it meant."

"I did you wrong. I meant well. I am sorry."

"If I did you wrong, I am not sorry!"

"But you are sorry for Iskinder." The najashi laughed again. "Well, if I can bring myself to send *you* away with my pardon, it is a small thing to overlook Iskinder's negligence into the bargain. When are you coming back to Himyar?"

"After your death! And not if I'm needed elsewhere first!"

"Good," said Abreha. "That's all I ask of you."

Telemakos blessed him. "God grant you a great long life of prosperity, and also many healthy children of your own, my najashi."

He meant it.

The Aksumite fleet was dismissed from al-Kabir. There was a change of guard at the prison, which Telemakos did not witness, because Priamos's ship was long departed before the military formalities were finished. The monsoon had not yet begun and the wind was still in their favor; they sped smoothly back to Adulis, running before the wind.

Telemakos slept contentedly through the dark, gentle nights of the sea voyage. His dreams were quiet and unmemorable, save one.

He knelt alone at a well in the Salt Desert, dipping up water in a small wooden cup. The cup was perfectly round, like a globe; it fit smoothly into the palm of Telemakos's single hand. When he looked inside it, the water was so clear he could see each grain of wood magnified, and the pattern made by these lines formed a miniature map of the world. Reflected light glinted here and there within the little hollow as though the map etched there was lit with tiny gold stars. When Telemakos lifted the cup to his lips he was astonished to find that the water of this barren place was sweet, and pure and cold as al-Surat mountain rain.

When Telemakos woke, he imagined the taste of this water lingered in his mouth.

"Peace to you, Lij Telemakos," said the familiar gatekeeper of the archon's mansion in the Aksumite port of Adulis. He bowed. "You've been lost. You have grown into a young warrior since you were here four years past!"

Turunesh was spinning flax in the basalt forecourt, expecting him. Telemakos knocked the bobbins flying across the glittering black pavement as he threw himself into her arms. Pandemonium broke loose as the white salukis joined him, competing wildly for his attention. Over his mother's shoulder, camouflaged among the black columns and tossing green fronds of the ornamental date palms, he could see a small figure following the salukis.

"Athena!" Telemakos cried out, reaching to her. "My Athena!"

She came tearing across the courtyard.

"Telemakos, *Telemakos!*"

She did not walk. She ran.

GLOSSARY

(G=Ge'ez, or ancient Ethiopic; A=Amharic, or
modern Ethiopian; SA=Sabaean, or ancient South Arabian;
MA=modern Arabian)

Amole (A): Block of cut salt used as currency.

Anbessa (G, A): Lion.

Bitwoded (A): Literally, "Beloved"; a bestowed, and unusual, noble title.

Emebet (A): Title for a young princess.

Hawri (MA): A narrow, open fishing boat, like a canoe.

Injera (A): Flat bread made from tef, Ethiopian grain.

Kat (MA): A mild stimulant in use throughout the Horn of Africa and the Arabian Peninsula. It grows as a small bush and the leaves are chewed fresh.

Kolo (A): Fried barley (eaten as a snack).

Lij (A): Title for a young prince (similar to European "childe").

Meskal (G, A): Feast of the Cross (literally "cross"), religious holiday taking place at the end of September.

Mukarrib (SA): Federator.

Najashi (SA): King.

Nebir (A): Leopard.

Ras (A): Title for a duke or prince.

Shamma (A): Cotton shawl worn over clothes by men and women.

Suq (MA): Market.

Tef (A): Ethiopian grain.

Wadi (MA): A valley, carved by rainwater runoff, that remains dry except in the rainy season.

Woyzaro (A): Title for a lady or princess.

ᚦAMILY TREE (Abreha)

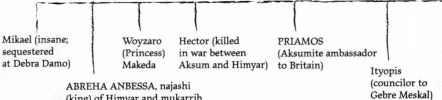

Mikael (insane;
sequestered
at Debra Damo)

Woyzaro
(Princess)
Makeda

Hector (killed
in war between
Aksum and Himyar)

PRIAMOS
(Aksumite ambassador
to Britain)

ABREHA ANBESSA, najashi
(king) of Himyar and mukarrib
(federator) of South Arabia

Ityopis
(councilor to
Gebre Meskal)

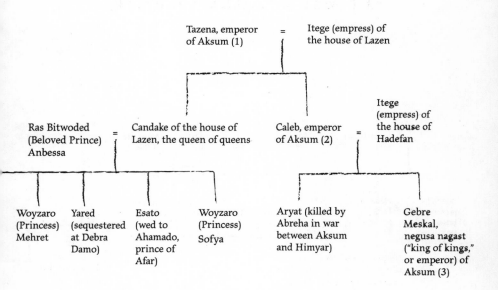

Tazena, emperor of Aksum (1) = Itege (empress) of the house of Lazen

Ras Bitwoded (Beloved Prince) Anbessa = Candake of the house of Lazen, the queen of queens

Caleb, emperor of Aksum (2) = Itege (empress) of the house of Hadefan

Woyzaro (Princess) Mehret

Yared (sequestered at Debra Damo)

Esato (wed to Ahamado, prince of Afar)

Woyzaro (Princess) Sofya

Aryat (killed by Abreha in war between Aksum and Himyar)

Gebre Meskal, negusa nagast ("king of kings," or emperor) of Aksum (3)

People with names in UPPER CASE letters appear in this book

ℱAMILY TREE (Telemakos)

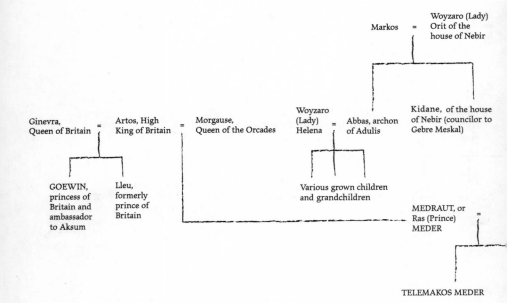

Markos = Woyzaro (Lady) Orit of the house of Nebir

Ginevra, Queen of Britain = Artos, High King of Britain = Morgause, Queen of the Orcades

Woyzaro (Lady) Helena = Abbas, archon of Adulis

Kidane, of the house of Nebir (councilor to Gebre Meskal)

GOEWIN, princess of Britain and ambassador to Aksum

Lleu, formerly prince of Britain

Various grown children and grandchildren

MEDRAUT, or Ras (Prince) MEDER =

TELEMAKOS MEDER

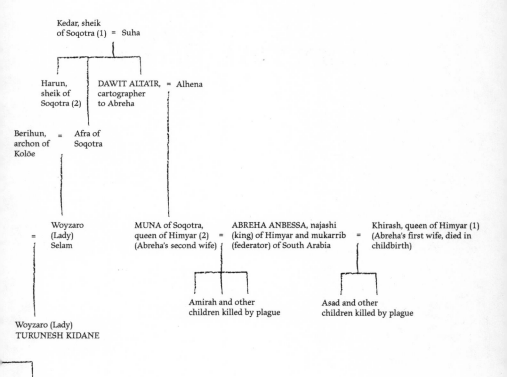

Kedar, sheik
of Soqotra (1) = Suha

Harun,
sheik of
Soqotra (2)

DAWIT ALTA'IR, = Alhena
cartographer
to Abreha

Berihun, = Afra of
archon of Soqotra
Kolöe

Woyzaro
(Lady)
Selam

MUNA of Soqotra,
queen of Himyar (2) =
(Abreha's second wife)

ABREHA ANBESSA, najashi
(king) of Himyar and mukarrib =
(federator) of South Arabia

Khirash, queen of Himyar (1)
(Abreha's first wife, died in
childbirth)

Amirah and other
children killed by plague

Asad and other
children killed by plague

Woyzaro (Lady)
TURUNESH KIDANE

ATHENA MEDER

People with names in UPPER CASE letters appear in this book

NOTE: the name of a "house" is carried through the female line. Telemakos inherits his family name, Nebir, through his mother Turunesh, but she takes the name from her father Kidane only because he has no sisters, and his wife, being of Arabian descent, does not belong to an Aksumite noble house. Telemakos is Kidane's heir, but if he has children they will be of their mother's house, not his. It is Athena's children who will preserve the name of the house of Nebir.

Elizabeth E. Wein was born in New York City and grew up in England, Jamaica, and Pennsylvania. She has a BA from Yale and a PhD from the University of Pennsylvania.

She has written four other novels in her ongoing Arthurian/Aksumite cycle: *The Winter Prince, A Coalition of Lions, The Sunbird,* and *The Lion Hunter* (the first book of the sequence called The Mark of Solomon).

Elizabeth Wein spent twenty-four years of her life as a student. She and her husband share a passion for maps, and they both fly small planes as private pilots. They live in Scotland with their two young children.

Visit her Web site at www.elizabethwein.com.